To raise his little girl up right was more than enough. He didn't need that special woman, after all.

Or so he'd believed until twelve nights ago.

Until Chloe led him into her house and straight to her bed.

Chloe.

She had it all—everything he'd already accepted he wasn't going to find. And no one had ever tasted so good.

Reluctantly, he broke the kiss.

She stared up at him, eyes full of stars. "Come back to my house? Be with me tonight?"

"Damn, Chloe. I was afraid you'd never ask."

* * *

THE BRAVOS OF JUSTICE CREEK:
Where bold hearts collide under Western skies

Dear Reader,

Chloe Winchester's perfect marriage crashed and burned. Now she's back in her hometown of Justice Creek, Colorado, starting over and determined to get it right this time.

Single dad Quinn Bravo has no interest in chasing women. He's got an adorable four-year-old daughter to raise and a growing business to run.

Once upon a time, Chloe was the town golden girl. Everyone knew she was destined for great things. Back then, Quinn was an angry, troubled boy, the one everyone thought was "slow," the one who was always getting in fights. Chloe used to avoid him then—even if, secretly, he made her heart beat faster. Quinn left town just after high school.

But now he's back in Justice Creek, too—and his house is just down the hill from hers. Neither of them is looking for love or romance. Chloe's been burned too badly. And Quinn just doesn't have the time.

But it only takes one fine, forbidden night with Chloe to have Quinn thinking he'd better *make* time...

Christine Rimmer

The Good Girl's Second Chance

Christine Rimmer

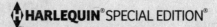

HARLEQUIN SPECIAL EDITION®

Recycling programs
for this product may
not exist in your area.

ISBN-13: 978-0-373-65913-5

The Good Girl's Second Chance

Copyright © 2015 by Christine Rimmer

Printed in U.S.A.

Christine Rimmer came to her profession the long way around. She tried everything from acting to teaching to telephone sales. Now she's finally found work that suits her perfectly. She insists she never had a problem keeping a job—she was merely gaining "life experience" for her future as a novelist. Christine lives with her family in Oregon. Visit her at christinerimmer.com.

For Kimberly Fletcher, aka Kimalicious,
Kimalovely, Kimhilarious—and more.
You warm my heart and make me smile.
I'm so happy to call you my friend.
And this one's for you!

Chapter One

Chloe Winchester woke with a startled cry.

She popped straight up in bed as her heart trip-hammered against her ribs. Splaying a hand to her heaving chest, she sent a frantic, frightened glance around the darkened room.

No threat. None.

Just her shadowed bedroom in the middle of the night, silvery moonlight streaming in the high, narrow window over the curtained sliding glass door.

"Nothing, it's nothing," she whispered aloud between gasps for air. "A nightmare." More specifically, it was *the* nightmare, the one starring her ultrasuccessful, über-controlling, bad-tempered ex-husband, Ted.

Not real, she reminded herself. Not anymore.

Ted Davies was the past. He held no threat for her now.

Chloe smoothed a shaking hand over her hair, pressed her cool fingers to her flushed cheek and took long, deep breaths until her racing heart slowed. Finally, when her pulse had settled to a normal rhythm and the dew of fear-sweat had dried on her skin, she plumped her pillow, settled back under the covers and closed her eyes.

Sleep didn't come.

She tossed and turned for a while, and then tried to make herself lie still as she stared up at the ceiling and willed herself to feel drowsy again.

Not happening.

Finally, with a weary sigh, she shoved back the covers and went to the kitchen. She heated milk and sweetened it with honey. Then she carried her mug to the living area, where she turned a single lamp on low. Gazing out the two stories of windows that faced her back deck, she sipped slowly and tried to clear her mind of everything but the beauty of the Colorado night.

She could see a light on in the big house down the hill from her. Quinn Bravo lived there with his little daughter, Annabelle, and that funny old guy, Manny. They'd moved in a few months before.

Chloe smiled to herself. So. Somebody down there couldn't sleep, either. Maybe Quinn? Could the tough martial arts star suffer from bad dreams, too?

Unlikely. Quinn "the Crusher" Bravo was world-famous for taking down the most unbeatable opponents. No mere nightmare would dare keep him awake. She wished she could be more like him, impervious and strong. He seemed so very self-confident in his quiet, watchful way.

And so different, really, from the boy he'd once been, the one she remembered from when they were children, the wild, angry boy with a chip the size of Denver on his shoulder who was always getting in fights.

Different also from the boy he'd become by high school, still rough-edged, but quieter, with a seething intensity about him. She'd avoided him then, the same as she had when they were children. All the nice girls avoided dangerous and unpredictable Quinn Bravo.

Even if, secretly, he made their hearts beat faster…

Quinn Bravo stood in his living room wearing an old pair of sweats, worn mocs and a Prime Sports and Fitness T-shirt. He stared blankly out the window at the faint gleam of light from the house up the hill. Beyond that house, the almost-full face of the moon hung suspended above the peaks of the Colorado mountains.

He should go back to bed. But he knew he wouldn't sleep. He couldn't stop thinking about what his four-year-old daughter had asked him when he tucked her in that night.

A faint movement beyond the wall of windows up the hill caught his eye. Must be Chloe. She lived there alone. Beautiful, smart Chloe Winchester, who'd gone off to college at Stanford and married some big-shot lawyer as everyone always knew she would. The big shot had carried her off to live the high life down in Southern California.

Quinn didn't know the whole story. He just knew that the marriage hadn't lasted. When he moved back to town several months ago, there was Chloe, minus the rich husband, with no kids, on her own in her old hometown, living in the shadow of the Rockies on the street up the hill from him.

Maybe a little fresh air would clear his head, relax him.

Quinn pulled open the French doors that led onto the back deck. It was a clear July night, almost balmy, the moon very close to full. He stepped outside and quietly shut the doors behind him. Crossing to the deck railing, he folded his arms across his chest, braced his legs wide and stared up at the light in Chloe's house. He indulged himself, allowing his mind to dwell on her a little, to wonder about her, about what might have messed up the smooth trajectory of her life and brought her back to Justice Creek alone.

True, it was none of his business, whatever had happened to bring Chloe back where she'd started. But focusing on what might have gone wrong for a woman he didn't really know took his mind off his little girl and her questions that he had no clue how to answer.

He noted movement again up there on the hill, a glass door sliding open.

And out she came, the one and only Chloe Winchester. Damn, she was gorgeous, even from a hundred yards away. Gorgeous, even in a baggy pink shirt. That long golden hair shone silvery in the moonlight and her fine, bare legs gleamed.

Quinn had no time for chasing women. He had a daughter to raise and a new business to build. But hot damn. Any man with a pulse would want to cut himself off a nice big slice of that.

Chloe went to the railing and rested her hands on it. For a long count of ten, she stared down at him as he looked up at her. She wasn't inviting him up exactly. But he definitely felt the pull.

And how could he help enjoying the moment? Hell. Chloe Winchester giving him the look? Never in a million years would he have guessed that would happen.

And the more they stared at each other, the more certain he became that a hundred yards was too much distance between them. He would much rather look at her up close. Manny was home if Annabelle woke up.

So he went back to the doors, pushed one open and engaged the lock, drawing it shut and hearing the click that meant his daughter was safe inside. When he turned again toward the woman up the hill, she hadn't moved. She remained at the railing, her head tipped slightly down and aimed in his direction, almost certainly watching him.

Fair enough, then.

He descended the back stairs, glancing up when he reached the bottom. She hadn't moved.

So he crossed his small patch of landscaped ground and began ascending the hill between their houses, skirting rocky outcroppings and ponderosa pines, the native grasses whispering beneath the leather soles of his mocs. He took it slow, glancing up at her now and then, expecting any moment that she would turn and retreat inside— at which point he would calmly wheel around and go home where he belonged.

But Chloe stood her ground.

When he reached the base of the stairs leading up to her deck, he paused, giving her a chance to…what?

Run away? Order him off her property?

When she only continued to gaze directly down at him, her eyes steady, her expression composed, he mounted the steps.

And she did move then. She came toward him, meeting him at the top where the steps opened wide. "Quinn," she said.

He nodded. "Chloe."

"Pretty night."

"Yeah, it is."

"How have you been?"

"Doing okay. You?"

A tiny smile flickered at the corner of her lush mouth. "Getting by." With that, she turned and led the way to a pair of cedar armchairs positioned close together in front of her great room windows. She dropped into one of those chairs, a move so graceful it stole his breath, and then gestured with a small, regal sweep of her hand for him to sit beside her.

He sat. And for several minutes, neither of them spoke. They stared up at the clear night sky and the milky smear of the faraway stars. The slight breeze brought her scent to him—like some exotic flower. Jasmine, maybe. And not only that, something…a little bit musky and a whole lot womanly.

Finally, she spoke again. "What keeps *you* awake, Quinn?" Her voice was low for a woman, low and calm and pleasing.

He turned and looked at her. Her eyes were a pale, glowing shade of blue, her face a smooth oval, that tempting mouth so soft and full. She really was a prize, every red-blooded man's fantasy of the perfect woman, a woman who would make a man a beautiful home and provide him with handsome, smart, upwardly mobile children.

And as to her question? He didn't plan to answer her. But then he opened his mouth and the truth fell out. "My daughter asked about her mother for the first time tonight. I'm trying to decide what to tell her."

Chloe hummed, a thoughtful sort of sound. "Her name is Annabelle, right?"

"That's right."

"So I'm assuming Annabelle doesn't know her mother?"

"No, she doesn't. I doubt she ever will."

"Ah." Chloe waited, her head tipped to the side, her eyes alert, giving him a chance to say more. When he remained silent, she suggested, "Tell her only the truth, but tell it carefully. She's how old?"

"Four."

"She wants to know that you love her. She wants to know she's safe and that her mother loves her, too—or would, if she knew her. She wants to know it's not her fault, whatever happened that you and her mother aren't together and her mother isn't in her life." Chloe smiled. God. What he wouldn't give to taste that mouth. "But don't load it on her all at once. Well-meaning parents have a tendency to overexplain. Try to get a sense of what she's ready for and just answer the questions she actually asks."

He faced front again and stared out at the night. She was so tasty to look at, with full breasts, the points of her nipples visible under that pink shirt. She had endless legs, slender arms and that perfect angel's face. He needed to take all that beauty in careful doses. He said, "I thought you didn't have kids."

"I don't. But I like kids." The beautiful voice was weighted with sadness. "Before I moved back home, I did volunteer day care with a San Diego family shelter. I helped out with special-needs children, too. And in college, I took just about every child development class available. I had big plans in college. I was going to be the perfect wife to a very important man—and the mother of at least three healthy, bright, happy children."

Strange. Looking away wasn't working for him. Why deprive himself of the sight of her? He turned his head and faced her once more, something down inside him going tight and hot when he met her eyes. "I remember you always seemed like you knew exactly where you were going."

"Yes, I did. I used to think I knew everything, used to be so sure of how my life would be." A husky chuckle escaped her. The sound rubbed along his nerve endings, stirring up sparks. "And that's what keeps *me* up nights, Quinn. All my big plans that came to dust..."

Somewhere in the distance, a coyote howled. Quinn

considered what, exactly, he ought to say next, if anything. He was still trying to find the right words when she stood.

He let his gaze track upward over those fine legs and her little pink terry-cloth shorts, over the womanly curves under the oversize shirt. The view was amazing. And he needed to thank her for the advice, say good-night and hustle his ass back down the hill.

But then she offered him her delicate, ladylike hand. He eyed it warily, glancing up again to meet those ice-blue eyes. No mistaking what he saw in those eyes: invitation.

It was the middle of the night and he didn't have time for this. He should be home in his own damn bed.

So, was he going to turn such beauty down?

Not. A. Chance.

He took the hand she offered. Her skin was cool and silky. Heat shot up his arm, down through the center of him and straight to his groin. Stifling a groan, he rose to stand with her.

She turned quickly, pulling him along behind her, pushing open the slider, leading him inside, across her two-story great room and down a short hall to her bedroom, which was as beautiful and tasteful as the woman herself, so feminine and orderly—except for the tangled covers on the unmade bed.

She bent and turned on the nightstand lamp, then stood tall to meet his eyes once more. "Somehow I feel…safe with you," she said in that fine alto voice that turned him on almost as much as her face and her body did. "I've noticed…" Her voice trailed away. She glanced down, swallowed and then, finally, raised her head to meet his gaze again.

He couldn't resist. He lifted a hand, nice and slow so

as not to spook her, and ran the back of his index finger along the silky skin of her throat. She trembled and sucked in a sharp little gasp of breath, but didn't duck away. And he asked, "You've noticed what?"

Her mouth twisted, as though the words were hard to come by. "Since you, uh, came back to town, you seem… I don't know. So calm. Kind of thoughtful. I admire that, I really do."

What could he say to that? Thanks? That seemed kind of lame, so he didn't say anything, just ran the back of his finger down the outside of her arm, enjoying the satiny feel of her skin, loving the way her mouth formed a soft O and her eyes went hazy in response to his touch.

She said, "I've been with one man in my life—my husband, who was supposed to be loving and tender and protective, but turned out to be one rotten, abusive, cheating SOB." She moved slightly away from him again, reaching over to pull open the bedside drawer. "I've been out a few times with nice men, in the year since I came home. I keep thinking I need to take the plunge again, take a chance again and be with someone new. So I bought these." She raised her hand and he saw that she held a strip of condoms. They unrolled from her palm with a snap. "To be prepared, you know?" A soft, rueful smile. "I haven't used a single one. I didn't want to. It never felt right. But tonight, with you… Quinn, I…" Her fine voice gone breathless, she said, "Back in high school, sometimes, I used to think about what it might be like, to be with you…"

Those words hit him right where he lived. "I used to think about you, too, Chloe."

Her amazing face glowed up at him. "You did?"

"Oh, yeah." Not that she ever would have gone out with him if he asked her. She'd had her plans for her life and they didn't include a wannabe cage fighter who could barely read. Plus, her snotty parents would've disowned her if she started in with one of Willow Mooney's boys, the ones they called the *bastard Bravos* because his mother hadn't married his father, Frank Bravo, until after Frank's rich first wife, Sondra, died.

Uh-uh. No way Linda Winchester would have let her precious only daughter get near him, one of Willow's boys—and the "slow" one, at that. And Chloe was always a good girl who did what her mama expected of her.

Chloe scanned his face, her expression suddenly anxious. "I have this feeling that somehow I should explain myself, give you a better reason to stay with me tonight..."

"Uh-uh." He stepped even closer—close enough that her body touched his. Her soft breasts brushed his chest, and the dizzying scent of her swam around him. Slowly, carefully, he lifted his hand and speared his fingers into that glorious mane of yellow hair. Like a curtain of silk, that hair. He loved the feel of it so much that he balled his fist and wrapped the thick strands around his wrist, pulling her even closer, right up against him, nice and tight.

"Oh!" she said on a shaky breath, baby blue eyes saucer-wide staring up into his.

All that softness and beauty, his for the night. He bent enough to suck in a deep breath through his nose. God, the scent of her. She smelled of everything womanly, everything most wanted—everything he'd never thought to hold, not even for a single night. He buried his face against her long, silky throat. "You don't need to explain anything, angel." He nuzzled her neck and then scraped his teeth across her tender skin. She gasped. He muttered, "Not a damn thing."

"I'm not an angel."

"Yeah, you are."

"Just for tonight, yeah?" She wrapped those slim arms around him, clutching him to her, tipping her head back, offering him more, offering him everything. "Just this one time…"

"However you want it."

"Just kiss me. Just…hold me. Just make me forget."

Chapter Two

Quinn took her by the shoulders and gently set her at arm's length. She swayed a little on her bare feet, gazing up at him, breathless, eyes starry with need.

He said, "First, I want to see you."

A soft gasp. "Okay."

"All of you."

"Okay."

He took her big pink shirt by the hem. "Raise your arms."

She obeyed without hesitation. He lifted the shirt up over her head, past the pink-painted tips of her fingers and tossed it away. Her hair settled, so shiny and thick, spilling past her shoulders, down her back, over her breasts. She let her arms fall back to her sides and gazed up at him expectantly.

Impossible. Chloe Winchester, naked to the waist, standing right in front of him.

He cupped one fine, full breast in his hand and flicked

the pretty nipple. His breath clogged in his throat, and the ache in his groin intensified. "You're so damn beautiful, Chloe."

"I…" She didn't seem to know what to say next. Which was fine. He was getting one night with her. And it wasn't going to be about what either of them might have to say.

He leaned close again, because he couldn't stop himself. He stuck out his tongue and licked her temple. She moaned. He blew on the place he'd just moistened, guiding her hair out of the way and whispering into the perfect pink shell of her ear "Take off those little shorts."

She whipped them down and off in an instant, so fast that he couldn't help smiling. And then she stood tall again, completely naked in front of him, an answering smile trembling its way across her mouth. "Quinn?"

"Shh. Let me look."

She widened her eyes—and then she shut them. And then she just stood there, eyes closed tight, and let him gaze his fill.

Touching followed. How could he help reaching for her? She was smooth and round and firm and soft. And she was standing right in front of him, Chloe Winchester, who had starred in more than one of his wild and impossible sexual fantasies when he was growing up.

He pulled her close again, wrapped his arms around the slim, yet curvy shape of her and pressed his lips into her hair. "Beautiful."

She lifted her face and gazed up at him. "You, too, please." He must have looked confused, because she added, "I want to see you, too."

He chuckled and stepped back. "Yes, ma'am." It took about ten seconds. He kicked off the mocs, reached back over his shoulders and pulled his shirt up and off. He eased the sweats over his erection and pushed them down, dropping them to the floor and stepping free of them.

"Oh," she said. "Oh, Quinn…" She reached out and ran her palm over his belly and then over the series of tats that covered his left arm. And then she touched the one for Annabelle, the angel's wings and the green vines, the trumpet flowers and his little girl's name, written right where it should be written, over his heart. "I never thought…you and me. Like this…?"

"Hey. Me, neither."

"Life can be so awful."

"Yeah."

"But then there are surprising, magical moments— like this one, huh?"

He nodded. "Yeah." He turned and shoved the tangled sheets and blankets out of the way. And then he took her by the waist, lifted her and set her on the bed. "Lie down."

She obeyed, stretching out on her side with a sigh. He went down to the mattress with her. He kissed her, tasting her mouth for the first time, finding it as sweet as the rest of her. Her tongue came out to play and for a while, they just lay there, on their sides, kissing and kissing, as if nothing else mattered in the whole damn world, nothing but his mouth and her mouth, the scrape of white teeth, the tangle of tongues.

One night they had together. He wanted to stretch every second just short of the breaking point, enjoy every touch, every sigh, every soft, tempting curve. He wanted to share her breath and the tender, urgent beat of her heart.

After he kissed her mouth, he kissed her everywhere else, too, taking forever about it, getting carried away, using his teeth as well as his tongue. He knew he left marks, marks he soothed with softer, gentler kisses. She never once objected when he used his teeth.

Far from it. She gasped and cried out her pleasure, clutching him close, telling him "Yes" and "More" and "Again, Quinn. Oh, again..."

He gave her more. More strokes, more kisses, trailing his mouth down the center of her, biting a little, trying not to be too rough, opening her, dipping his tongue in. He pushed her legs wide and settled between them for a long time.

She came twice then, as he played her with his mouth and his hands. She had his name on her lips, over and over. He loved that most of all: Chloe Winchester, calling his name as she came.

After that second time, when she was boneless and open for him, he rose to his knees between her spread thighs. Ripping the first condom off the strip, he took off the wrapper and rolled it down over his length, easing it into place nice and tight. She stared up at him, dazed and flushed and softly smiling.

"Quinn." She reached for him. "Please..."

And he went down to her, taking most of his weight on his arms. She slipped her hand between them, closing those slim fingers around him. He was the one groaning then, the one calling *her* name.

She guided him in. He sank into her slowly, carefully, little by little, stretching her and the moment, making it last. She felt so good—better than anything he'd ever known, soft and welcoming, and a little bit tight.

He varied the rhythm, watching her face, matching his strokes to her pleasured moans, her hungry cries. Somehow he stayed with her, until she went over for the third time. After that, there was no holding back. He was rough and fast, and she clung to him, nice and tight, all the way to the peak and over the edge.

She cradled him close then, stroking his shoulders and his arms, whispering "So good. Just right," laughing a little. "Who knew, really? Whoever would have thought…?"

"Beautiful," he said. "Never would have guessed."

They must have dozed for a while.

He woke to find her sleeping peacefully, one arm across his chest. He'd been hoping that maybe they would have time to play some more.

But it was later than he'd thought. The clock by the bed said 5:05 in the morning. The first glow of daylight would be bleeding the night from the sky all too soon. The houses in their neighborhood were spaced far apart, built to conform to the shape of the land, with plenty of big trees between them. He might make it down the hill in broad daylight with no one the wiser.

But why take that chance? It was nobody's business, this one unforgettable night they'd shared.

With care, he eased out from under her arm. She sighed and rolled to her back, but didn't wake. He slid from the bed. Before settling the covers over her, he stole another long glance at her and got struck by a last hot bolt of pure lust at the sight of the faint marks he'd left on her perfect breasts, her pretty belly.

They would fade soon, those marks. He tried not to wish…

Uh-uh. Never mind. One night. That was the deal.

He pulled on his clothes and went out the way he'd come in, noting that she hadn't rearmed the alarm on the wall by the slider when she led him inside.

Good. That meant he didn't have to wake her to go. He locked the slider and then went out through the front door, which he could also lock behind him, thus securing her inside.

He ran around the side of the house and then on down the hill.

At home, he got the spare key from its hiding place under the stairs and let himself in. The house was just as he'd left it. Silent and dark.

He stepped inside and shut the doors with barely a sound—and found Manny, his former trainer and longtime business partner, sitting in one of the big chairs by the moss rock fireplace. The old fighter switched on the lamp beside him. He wore a knowing grin on that roadmap of a face. "Hey, Crush. Where you been?"

Quinn locked the doors. "Since when are you my mother?"

Manny rumbled out a low laugh. "You and that gorgeous uptown blonde up the hill? I never had a clue."

"I don't know what you're talkin' about." Quinn headed for the stairs.

Manny watched him go. "She's a fine one. I find I am lookin' at you with new respect."

"Night, Manny."

"Got news for you, Crush. It's tomorrow already."

Quinn just kept walking. Manny's knowing cackle followed him up the stairs.

Chloe was sound asleep when her alarm went off at seven.

She woke with a smile, feeling thoroughly rested and a little bit sore. If it weren't for that soreness and the small, already-fading red marks and bruises on her breasts and stomach, she almost might have been able to tell herself that the night before was all a dream.

Not that she wanted to deny what had happened. It had been glorious. She'd loved every minute of it.

As she sat up and stretched, yawning with gusto, she couldn't help wishing she hadn't told Quinn that she only wanted one night. Because he was remarkable. He'd given her hope that love and passion and tenderness weren't all just some fantasy, some bright, naive dream that could never come true.

She would love to spend more time with him.

But she let her arms drop and her shoulders droop with a sigh.

No. They had a deal and she would stick by it. He'd been great and the sex had been mind-blowing. Now she knew for certain that there were better lovers out there than Ted. She would be grateful for that and eventually, maybe, she'd find someone who made her want to take another chance on forever.

She got ready for work and then had breakfast. The house phone rang just as she was heading out the door. Probably her mother. She'd check her messages later and call her back then.

As she was pulling out of the driveway, her cell rang. She slipped the SUV into Park and checked the display. With a sigh, she gave in and answered. "Hi, Mom. Just on my way over to the showroom."

"But it's not even nine yet," Linda Winchester complained. "You have time to stop by the house. Let me fix you some breakfast."

"I've already eaten. And I have to get the shop opened."

"Sweetheart, it's your shop. You're the boss. No need to rush over there at the crack of dawn."

"Come on, Mom. A successful business doesn't run itself." Not that Your Way Interior Design was all that successful. Yet.

"I hardly see you lately. We need to chat."

Chatting with her mother was the *last* thing she needed. They hadn't been getting along all that well since Chloe's divorce. And it had only gotten worse after she returned to Justice Creek. Linda knew what was right for her only child and she never missed an opportunity to lecture Chloe on all she'd done wrong. And somehow, whenever they "chatted," her mother always managed to bring up Ted and the perfect life Chloe had thrown away. "Mom, I'll have to call you later. I need to get to work."

"But, sweetheart, I want to—"

"Call you tonight, Mom."

Her mother was still protesting as Chloe disconnected the call.

She drove to her showroom and unlocked the doors at nine, an hour before most of the businesses on Central Street opened. She had a good location and an attractive shop, with neutral walls and sleek, modern cabinetry and red and yellow accents to give it energy and interest. Her motto was Your Space, Your Way. She had attractive displays, and plenty of them, lots of table space for spreading out samples. And she was trained in every aspect of home design, from blueprints up.

Her website looked great and she stayed active on Facebook, Pinterest, Twitter and Tumblr. She kept a blog where she gave free tips on great ways to spiff up your living space. During the school year, she ran a workshop right there in her showroom for high school students interested in interior design. She contributed her expertise to local churches, helping them spruce up their Sunday school rooms and social halls. And she worked right along with the other shop owners in Justice Creek on various chamber of commerce projects.

Still, it took time to build a business. Chloe had found

a real shark of a divorce lawyer who'd put the screws to Ted and got her a nice lump settlement, which Chloe had asked for. The onetime payout was less than monthly alimony would have been in total, but the last thing she wanted was to be getting regular checks from Ted. With the settlement, she'd been able to cut ties with him completely.

She'd tried to spend her money wisely. She loved her house, which she'd redone herself, and she was proud of her business. But the past couple of months, she had more to worry about than putting Ted behind her and whether or not there might someday be love in her future.

Chloe's nest egg was shrinking. Your Way needed to start paying *its* way.

That day, as it turned out, was better than most. She had steady walk-in traffic. A new couple in town came in and hired her to do all the window treatments in the house they'd just bought. She scheduled three appointments to give estimates: two living room redesigns and a kitchen upgrade. When her assistant, Tai Stockard, a design student home from CU for the summer, came in at one, Chloe sent her to the Library Café for takeout paninis. It was turning into a profitable day and they might as well enjoy a nice lunch.

Chloe went home smiling—until she remembered she owed her mother a call.

"Come on over for dinner," her mother coaxed. "I've got lamb chops and twice-baked potatoes just the way you love them. We're leaving for Maui tomorrow." Chloe's mom and dad would be gone for two weeks, staying at a luxury resort where her mother could enjoy the spa and the lavish meals and her father could play golf. "I want to see you before we go."

Chloe went to dinner at the house where she'd grown

up. It wasn't that bad. Linda managed not to say a single word about Ted. And it was good to see her dad. An orthodontist with a successful practice, Doug Winchester had a dry sense of humor and never tried to tell his only daughter how to live her life.

By nine, Chloe was back at home. She got ready for bed, settled under the covers with the latest bestseller and tried not to let her mind wander to the question of what Quinn Bravo might be doing that night.

Quinn heard the soft whisper of small feet across the tiled floor as he stared out the window at the single light shining from inside Chloe's house. "Go back to bed, Annabanana," he said softly without turning.

"I can't."

"Why not?"

"The monsters are very noisy. And I'm not a banana. You know that, Daddy."

"Yes, you are." He turned and dropped to a crouch. "You're my favorite banana."

Dragging her ancient pink blanket and her one-eyed teddy bear, Annabelle marched right up to him and put one of her little hands on his shoulder. "No, I'm not. I'm a *girl*."

He leaned closer and whispered, "Ah. Gotta remember that."

"Pick me up, Daddy," she instructed. "Get the flashlight."

He wrapped his arms around her and stood. She giggled and hugged his neck, shoving her musty old teddy bear into the side of his face. He detoured to the kitchen, where he got the flashlight from a drawer. Then he returned to the living room and mounted the stairs.

She didn't object as he carried her up to her room, set

her down on the bed, flicked on the lamp and then pulled the covers up over her and the stuffed bear, smoothing the ancient blanket atop her butterfly-printed bedspread.

"Closet," she said, when he bent to kiss her plump cheek.

He went to the closet, pushed the door open and shone the light around inside. "Nothing in here."

"You have to tell them," she said patiently. "You know that."

He ran the light over her neatly hung-up dresses and the row of little shoes and said in his deepest, gruffest voice, "Monsters, get lost." He rolled the door shut. "That should do it."

But Annabelle didn't agree. "Now under the bed."

So he knelt by the bed and lifted up the frilly bed skirt and shone the light around underneath. "Holiday Barbie's down here. With her dress over her head."

The bed skirt on the other side rustled as small hands lifted it and Annabelle appeared, upside down. "Oops." She snatched up the doll and let the bed skirt drop. "Okay, tell them."

"Monsters, get lost." He gave a long, threatening growl for good measure. On the bed, his daughter laughed, a delighted peal of sound that had him smiling to himself. "So, all right," he said. "They're gone." And then he got up and sat on the bed and tucked her in again, bending close to press a kiss on her cheek and breathe in the little-girl smell of her. Toothpaste and baby shampoo, so familiar. So sweet. "Anything else?" he asked, suddenly worried about how she might answer, recalling Chloe's wise advice of the night before. *She wants to know it's not her fault, whatever happened that you and her mother aren't together and her mother isn't in her life…*

Annabelle shook her head. "That's all."

He felt equal parts guilt and relief. Guilt that he wasn't as good a father as Annabelle deserved. Relief that he wouldn't have to tackle the tough questions tonight, after all. "You know there are really no monsters in your room, right?"

She nodded slowly. "But I like it when you scare them away."

He got up. "Sleep now, princess."

She beamed at him. "Princess is good. Not banana."

"Close your eyes…"

"I want a princess room. All the princesses. Snow White and Cinderella and Mulan and Elsa and Belle and Merida and—"

"Time for sleep. Close your eyes…" He heard Chloe's rich alto again, as though she whispered in his ear. *She wants to know that you love her.* "I love you, princess."

"Love you, Daddy." With a little sigh, Annabelle closed her eyes. He turned off the light and shut the door silently behind him on the way out.

Back downstairs, all was quiet. Manny had gone to Boulder for the night to visit his current lady friend. Quinn took up his vigil at the wall of windows in the living room. Up at Chloe's the light remained on. He could see it glowing through the pale curtains that covered the slider in her bedroom. He pictured her, wearing that big pink shirt, propped up against the pillows in her bed, with her laptop or maybe a good book, which she would read effortlessly, turning the pages fast to find out what would happen next.

And then, well, after last night, he couldn't help picturing her other ways—like, say, naked beneath him, moaning his name in that low, sexy voice that drove him crazy. He told himself it was a good thing that Manny wasn't there to watch over Annabelle if he stepped out.

Because climbing that hill again?

Way too much on his mind.

"Crush, I gotta say it," Manny grumbled. "I'm disappointed in you."

It was Friday night, five nights since the one Quinn had spent with Chloe. Annabelle had been tucked safely in bed, the monsters chased away. Quinn and Manny sat out on the deck having a beer under the clear, starry sky. Quinn took a long, cool swallow and said nothing.

Manny wiggled his white eyebrows. They grew every which way and he never bothered to trim them. "Aren't you gonna ask me why?"

Quinn gave a low chuckle. "We both know you'll tell me anyway."

Manny snorted. "Yes, I will. I've spent over a decade makin' sure you learn what you need to know. No reason to change now."

Quinn only looked at him, waiting.

Manny announced, "Romance is like everything else worth doin' in life. You gotta follow up, put some energy into it, or it goes nowhere."

"I don't know why you're telling *me* this."

"I'll give you a hint. Chloe Winchester. Only a fool would pass up his chance with a woman like that."

"That's given that he *had* a chance in the first place."

"See there? That's defeat talkin'. Quinn the Crusher, he spits in the face of defeat."

"Quinn the Crusher retired, remember?"

"From the Octagon, sure. But not from life. Last time I checked, you still got a pulse."

"Leave it alone, Manny."

Manny did no such thing. "A woman like that, she lets you in her house in the middle of the night, you got a chance. You got more than a chance."

"You need to stop sticking your nose in where it doesn't belong. Somebody's likely to break it."

"Won't be the first time." A raspy cackle. "Or the second or the third." Manny swiped a gnarled, big-knuckled hand back over his buzz cut and then took a pull off the longneck in his other fist. "I will repeat. Momentum is everything."

Quinn got up from his deck chair and headed for the French doors. "Night, Manny."

"Where you going?"

"I'm halfway through *A Tale of Two Cities*." He had it in audio book, and tried to get in a few chapters a night. Little by little, he was working his way through the great books of Western literature.

Manny wasn't impressed with Quinn's highbrow reading. "It's just dandy, you improving your mind and all, but a man needs more than a book to keep him warm at night."

There was no winning an argument with Manny. Quinn knew that from years of experience. "Lock up when you come in." He stepped inside and shut the doors before the old fighter could get going again.

The following Monday, Chloe was selling new carpet to Agnes Oldfield, a pillar of the Justice Creek community and a longtime friend of her mother's, when who should walk in the door but Manny Aldovino? Quinn's little girl was with him, looking like a pint-size princess in an ankle-length dress with a hot pink top, a wide white sash at the waist and a gathered cotton skirt decorated with rickrack in a rainbow of bright colors.

Chloe ignored the fluttering sensation beneath her breastbone that came with being reminded of Quinn, and greeted the newcomers with a cheery "Hi, Manny. Annabelle. Have a look around. I'll be right with you. Crayons and paper in the hutch by the window treatment display, in case Annabelle would like to color. And there's coffee, too." She gestured at the table not far from the door.

"Sounds good," said Manny. He winked at Agnes. "How you doin' there, Agnes?"

"Mr. Aldovino." Agnes gave Manny an icy, dismissive nod. She'd always been a terrible snob and she looked down on anyone she didn't consider of her social standing. Also, Quinn's father's first wife, Sondra, had been Agnes's beloved niece. Agnes thoroughly disapproved of Quinn's mother, Willow, and of all of Willow's children. Now Agnes pointedly turned her back on Manny and said to Chloe, "Please continue, dear."

Agnes's attitude could use adjusting. But Chloe reminded herself that she needed the business and she couldn't afford to offend a customer. She sent Manny an apologetic smile and waited on the old woman, who wanted new carpet for three rooms. She'd already settled on a quality plush in a pretty dove gray. Chloe accepted her deposit and gave her the number to call to arrange a time to have the spaces measured.

In her eighties, Agnes always dressed as though she'd been invited to tea with the Queen of England. She adjusted the giant, jeweled lizard brooch on her pink silk Chanel suit and said, "Thank you, my dear."

"Have a great day, Agnes."

The old lady sailed out the door.

"Wound a little tight, that one," Manny remarked drily once Agnes was gone.

With a sigh and a shrug, Chloe joined the old man

and the little girl at one of the worktables. "Now. What can I do for you?"

Annabelle glanced up from coloring an enormous, smiling yellow sun. Chloe saw Quinn in the shape of his daughter's eyes and the directness of her gaze. Really, the little girl was downright enchanting, with that heart-shaped face and those chipmunk cheeks. Chloe felt a bittersweet tug at her heartstrings. Annabelle reminded her of the children she should have had.

But after that first time Ted punched her, having kids had never felt right. And Ted hadn't really cared about children anyway. He wanted his wife focused on him.

"I want a princess room," the little girl announced. Chloe gladly put away her grim thoughts of Ted to focus on the sprite in the darling dress. "Manny says you can make me one."

"Yes, I can."

"I want *all* the princesses. Belle and Merida and—" Manny chuckled and tapped the little girl on the arm. She glanced up at him. "But, Manny—"

"I know, I know. You want all the princesses and you're gonna get 'em, but what did we talk about?"

Annabelle huffed. "To wait my turn and not be rude."

The old man beamed. "That's right."

Annabelle leaned close to him, batted those big eyes and whispered, "But I want my princess room."

"It's yours. Promise. But the grown-ups have to talk now."

"Okay." Annabelle bent to her smiling sun again.

Manny spoke to Chloe then. "Quinn's pretty busy getting the business off the ground." His gym, Prime Sports and Fitness, was just down the street from Chloe's showroom, at the intersection of West Central and Marmot Drive. "You know Quinn, don't you?"

"Of course. We…went to school together."

"Right. So Quinn takes care of the business. I look after Annabelle and run the house. You ever seen the inside of our house?"

Chloe blinked away a mental image of Quinn, up on his knees between her legs. Quinn, gloriously naked, his beautiful blue-green eyes burning down at her. "Erm, your house? No, I haven't been inside."

"It's a good house, big rooms, great light, four thousand square feet. But built in the eighties, and looks like it. Too much ceramic tile and ugly carpet."

"So it needs a little loving care?" she asked, trying to sound cool and professional and fearing the old man could see right inside her head to the X-rated images of Annabelle's dad.

"What it needs is a boatload of cash and a good decorator. Starting on the ground floor and moving on up."

"You want to redo every room?" That would be good for her. Very good. Not only for the money, but for Your Way's reputation. She could put up a whole new website area, if Quinn and Manny agreed, showing the before and after of at least the main rooms. Their housing development was an upscale one. However, like Quinn's house, most of the homes were more than twenty years old. Doing a full-on interior redesign always got the neighbors' attention, got them thinking that their houses could stand a little sprucing up, too. She could end up with a lot of new business from the job Manny described. She asked, "What about the bathrooms and the kitchen?"

"Like I said, all of it. Every room."

She couldn't help wondering if Quinn was behind this? "What will you need from me? I'll be happy to show you examples of my work—my portfolio? We can take a look at the website so you'll have a better feel of what I can do. As for references, I—"

"Naw. I already looked at the website and I liked what I saw."

Was she blushing? Manny had a gruff way about him, but he also knew how to turn on the charm. She really liked him. She liked his way with Annabelle, liked that teasing twinkle in his watery eyes. "Well, thank you."

"I got a good feeling about you, Chloe. A real good feeling." The old guy smiled, deepening the network of wrinkles on his craggy face. She really did wonder exactly how much he knew about her and Quinn and what had happened between them eight nights ago. He went on. "I'm thinking you should come over to the house. I'll show you around, show you what I want done and then you can come up with some drawings and blueprints and all that. We can start right away, as soon as you're ready to go…"

"Do you have an architect or any contractors you want to use?"

"Bravo Construction, if they give you a decent bid on the job—and if you're okay with them. You'll be running this, so you gotta be happy with the people you're working with."

Chloe nodded. "I know them, of course." Quinn's older brother, Garrett, ran the company, from what Chloe had heard. And his youngest sister, Nell, worked there, too. Garrett had been three years or so ahead of Chloe in school, so she didn't remember all that much about him. And Nell was four years younger than Chloe. Still, Chloe vaguely remembered her. Gorgeous, and something of a wild child, wasn't she? Never one to back down from a fight. She told Manny brightly, "They have a great reputation. I'll ask them for a bid, absolutely."

Manny winked at her. "Might as well try and keep it in the family."

Chloe got the message. Manny did want her to use the Bravos. "Sounds good to me." She made a mental note to go with them if at all possible.

Half an hour later, when Manny and Annabelle left, Chloe had an appointment at Quinn's house for two in the afternoon the next day.

She was thrilled.

But then again, come on. It was too much of a coincidence. She suspected rough-edged old Manny of matchmaking, because it just didn't seem like something Quinn would engineer. Quinn Bravo was more direct than that. If he wanted to see her again, he would just say so.

Wouldn't he?

She had to admit she couldn't be sure. Maybe Quinn hesitated to ask her out now, after she'd made such a point of that one night being the *only* night the two of them would ever share.

Maybe he knew nothing about Manny's plans to tear their house apart and redo it, top to bottom.

Maybe, come to think of it, Quinn had no desire at all to ask her out. What if he ended up hating the idea that his daughter's caregiver planned to hire the woman up the hill, with whom he'd had a one-night stand? What if he wanted nothing to do with her now? If she took the job, she would be in and out of his house for weeks.

That would be awful, if it turned out that Quinn really didn't want her around. Here she was, gloating over this plum job that had magically fallen in her lap, when Quinn might know nothing about it—and not be the least bit happy when he found out.

By the time Tai arrived at one, Chloe had made up her mind.

Before she went to Quinn's house tomorrow and consulted with Manny on the changes he wanted made, she needed to know for sure what Quinn really thought of her being there.

And the only way to know for sure was to ask the man himself.

Chapter Three

Chloe sent Tai to get takeout again. They shared lunch. And then she left Tai in charge and walked the two blocks to Prime Sports and Fitness, her heart hammering at her ribs all the way.

Quinn's gym filled a three-story brick building directly across the street from the popular Irish-style pub, McKellan's. Chloe hesitated outside on the sidewalk, ordering her pulse to slow down a little, noting the good location and the clean, modern lines of the building itself. There were lots of windows and various athletic activities visible from the street. In one room, some kind of martial arts class was in progress. Another room took up most of the second floor and held rows of cardio equipment, with people in exercise gear working out on stationary bikes, treadmills and elliptical trainers.

She stood there staring up for a couple of minutes at least. Until she finally had to accept that her nervousness hadn't faded at all. In fact, it was worse. So she smoothed the front of her narrow white pants, tugged on the hem of the light, short blazer she wore over a featherweight black tank, squared her shoulders and went in.

The gorgeous, hardbody brunette at the front desk said that Quinn was just finishing up leading a boxing conditioning class. Chloe could wait in his office. It shouldn't be long.

So Chloe sat in his office, where the walls were lined with pictures of Quinn in his fighting days and more than one big, shiny trophy stood on display. She had become absolutely certain that she'd made a horrible mistake in coming here and was just about to rise and bolt from the building, when the door swung open and there he was, looking sweaty and spectacular in gray boxing shorts and a muscle-hugging T.

"Hello, Chloe." Quinn thought he'd never seen anyone so smooth and beautiful, in those perfect white pants and pointy little shoes, not a single golden hair out of place.

"Quinn." She sounded breathless. He liked that. And she bounced to her feet. "I... How are you?" She held out her hand.

"Good. Real good." He stepped forward and took it, already regretting he hadn't run to the locker room and grabbed a quick shower after class. Her slim fingers were cool and dry in his sweaty paw.

But she didn't seem to mind. She held on and he held on and they stood and stared at each other. She looked a little stunned, but in a good way. And he had no doubt his expression mirrored hers.

Finally, she said in a breathless rush, "I need... Well, there's something I really have to discuss with you."

"Sure." He made himself release her hand and went

back to shut the door as she returned to the chair. "Something to drink? Juice? Tea?" When she shook her head, he slid in behind his desk and gestured for her to sit back down. "Okay. What's going on?"

"I, uh, had a visit from Manny and Annabelle today, at my design showroom. Manny offered me a really good project, redoing all the rooms in your house." She paused to swallow and smooth her already perfect hair. "I agreed to meet him at your house tomorrow in the afternoon to go over the changes he wants. If he still wants to hire me, I'll work out the numbers and put together a contract."

This was all news to Quinn. But not bad news. He asked cautiously, "And this is a problem somehow?"

"Well, after Manny and Annabelle left, I started wondering if you even knew that he was planning to hire me. I thought I should, you know, check with you, make certain you're on board with Manny's plan..." Her voice trailed off.

He watched her try not to fidget. And the longer he sat there looking at her, the more he came to grips with the fact that the one night he'd had with her wasn't enough. Luckily for him, her signal came through loud and clear: she felt the same way.

No, he had no time for romance.

But for a woman like Chloe, he might just have to make time.

Should he be pissed off at Manny for taking the situation into his battered old hands? Probably. Manny had no business butting in.

But Quinn had just spent a week keeping himself from climbing the hill to get to her. Manny's bold move had brought her right to him. Pissed off? Hardly. Downright grateful was more like it.

Not that he'd ever admit that to Manny.

A small, embarrassed sound escaped her. "Oh, God. You *didn't* know, did you?"

"Doesn't matter. Manny's in charge of the house and we agreed when we bought the place that it would need major upgrades. It's his call who he hires to make that happen."

"So you're okay with it—with me, working in your house?"

He was more than just okay with it. "Sounds like a good idea to me—I mean, if you're willing."

She gave him one of those glowing smiles that could light up the blackest night. "Well, then. Yes. I'm willing, definitely." She got up. "So, then, I guess I should be..."

He couldn't let her go. Not yet. He pushed back his chair. "Now that you're here, how 'bout I show you around?"

"The gym, you mean?"

"That's right."

"Yes. Yes, I would like that."

"Well, okay, then. This way..."

Chloe followed Quinn past the reception area, into a series of wood-floored classrooms with mirrored walls and different kinds of equipment stacked in the corners. In one, a fitness ball class was in progress. In another, the participants were paired up for intense stretching. They went upstairs to the second floor and the giant cardio room as well as a room with all kinds of weight machines and one with boxing equipment and two rings.

He explained that Prime Fitness tried to offer something for everyone. "We have martial arts for all ages, boxing, kickboxing, general fitness and yoga classes..."

She listened and nodded, just glad to be walking along

beside him, glad that he seemed to want to keep her there longer, to be drawing the moments out before she left.

On the top floor there was a beginning women's self-defense class in progress. They watched through the observation window as a big guy in a padded suit tried to take down a woman about Chloe's size. The woman shouted and fought him off violently, kicking and slugging at him, spinning away and sprinting off as soon as she got the guy to let go of her.

Watching that made Chloe's mouth go dry and her palms feel clammy. It made her think of Ted and how she ought to be better prepared if anyone ever hit her or threatened her again.

"What do you think?" Quinn asked.

She turned to him, met those wonderful, watchful eyes. "I think I might want to take a class like this."

There was a bench a few feet away. He backed up and sat down. She left the viewing window and sat beside him.

He said, "This class is wrapping up. A new one will start next week, and there's an evening class, too. Starts in two weeks. It's an eight-week course, one two-hour class per week."

"I'll be fighting off guys in padded suits for eight weeks?"

He shook his head. "No. Initially there are sessions on staying out of violent confrontations in the first place."

"How?"

He chuckled. "What? You want an outline of the course?"

"Can you give me one?"

"You're serious?"

"I am, yes."

He watched her for a long moment. And then he shrugged. "Well, all right. The class starts with a section on the nature of predators. Basically there are two types. Resource and process. Resource predators want your stuff. Process predators are in it for the power and the thrill. They want to mess you over. They actually enjoy committing crimes. The class shows you how to identify what kind of scumbag you're faced with and how to deal with him. Next comes a study of avoidance, because the best option is always steering clear of any situation where you could get hurt. After avoidance, there's a section on deescalating conflict. If you can't escape trouble before it happens, the second-best option is to diffuse it. And finally you'll learn how to fight off an attack."

"Wow," she said, and wondered if any guy ever looked as good in shorts and a T-shirt as Quinn did. And he smelled so good, too. Clean. Just sweaty enough to be exciting…

He grunted. "See? More information than you needed or wanted."

She shook her head. "That was exactly what I wanted to know. And how do *you* know all that? Do you teach this kind of class yourself?"

"No. But I've been through every class that we offer here. I run the place. It's my job to know what I'm selling. I want to franchise this operation. This location will be the model for Prime Sports and Fitness gyms all over the country."

"You dream big."

"Hey. Balls to the wall. It's the only way to go."

She made a decision. "I'm taking the next evening class."

"Am I a salesman, or what?" He got up. "Come on." He put his big hand at the small of her back. Such a light touch to wreak such total havoc through every quivering cell in her body. "We'll sign you up."

At the front desk, Quinn tried to comp her the class. She shook her head and whipped out her checkbook. Once she'd paid for the course, he walked her out the door.

He caught her arm as the door eased shut behind them. "So, Chloe…"

She was achingly aware of him, so close, his big, warm fingers wrapped lightly around her upper arm. He walked her forward several feet along the sidewalk and then pulled her gently around to face him.

"Yeah?" she asked low, her voice barely a whisper.

He stepped in closer and spoke for her ears alone. "The other night…?"

Her breath tangled in her throat. "Yeah?"

"You said just for that night, just that once. But you're here and I'm looking in those fine blue eyes and I'm wondering, did you really mean that?"

Her stupid throat had clutched up tight. She swallowed convulsively, and then shook her head hard.

His brow rumpled in a frown, but the hint of a smile seemed to tug on his mouth. "I'm still not sure what you're telling me here."

And somehow she found her voice again. "Sorry…"

"Nothing to be sorry for. You just say it right out loud, whatever your answer is. I can take it, I promise you."

She cleared her throat to get her going. "Ahem. That night, I needed to find a way to give myself permission to do something I wanted to do but had never done before. That night, I needed to think of it as just that one time and never again. But since then…"

"Yeah?"

"Oh, Quinn. I wish I hadn't said what I said. Because I've been thinking about you a lot. And it's really good to see you again."

Those fine eyes were gleaming. "Yeah?"

And she was eagerly nodding, her head bouncing up and down like a bobblehead doll's.

"So, then..." He started walking backward toward the doors.

She resisted the urge to reach out and stop him—and also the one that demanded she follow him. Instead, she held her ground and asked hopefully, "So, then, what?"

He stopped at the doors. "How 'bout Friday night? You and me. Dinner."

"Dinner..." How could one simple word hold so much promise?

"Yeah." He was definitely smiling now. "You know, like people do."

"I would like that." She knew she wore a giant, silly grin. And somehow she had gone on tiptoe. Her body felt lighter than air.

"Pick you up at seven?"

She settled back onto her heels and nodded. "Seven is great."

A trim, fortyish woman in workout clothes approached the doors. Quinn opened one and ushered her in. Then, with a final nod in Chloe's direction, he went in, too.

That lighter-than-air feeling? It stayed with her. Her feet barely touched the ground the whole way back to the showroom.

Strange how everything could change for the better in the course of one afternoon.

All at once, the world, so cruel to her in recent years, was a good and hopeful place again. Suddenly everything looked brighter.

Yeah, okay. It was just a date. But it was a date with a man who thrilled her—and made her feel safe and protected and cherished and capable, all at the same time.

* * *

That night, Chloe made chocolate chip cookies. Once they'd cooled, she packed them up into two bright decorator tins. She took them to the showroom the next morning. One she offered at the coffee table.

The other she carried with her when she went to meet with Manny at Quinn's house after lunch.

"Cookies!" Annabelle nodded her approval. "I *like* cookies." She sent Manny a regretful glance. "Manny's cookies are not very good."

Manny told Chloe, "Never was a baker—or that much of a cook, when you come right down to it. I enjoy cooking, though. Too bad nobody appreciates my efforts." He wiggled his bushy eyebrows at Annabelle. "And what do you say when someone brings you really good cookies?"

"Thank you, Chloe."

"You're welcome."

She turned those sweet brown eyes on Manny again. "Can I have one now?"

"That could be arranged." Manny led them to the kitchen, which had appliances that had been state-of-the-art back in the late eighties, a fruit-patterned wallpaper border up near the ceiling and acres of white ceramic tile. Annabelle made short work of two cookies and a glass of milk, after which she wanted to take Chloe up to her room.

Chloe looked to Manny. The old guy shrugged. "Don't keep her up there all day," he said to the little girl.

"Manny, I want *all* the princesses, but it won't take *that* long." She reached right up and grabbed Chloe's hand, at which point Chloe's heart pretty much melted. "Okay, Chloe. Let's go."

After half an hour with Quinn's daughter, Chloe knew exactly which princesses Annabelle wanted represented in her new room, as well as her favorite colors. They went back downstairs, and Chloe spent a couple of hours with Manny, going through the house, bottom to top, talking hard and soft surfaces, color choices, style preferences and the benefits of knocking out a wall or two. Chloe jotted notes and took pictures of existing furniture and fixtures that would be included in the new design.

Before she left at four-thirty, she promised to crunch the numbers. The contract would be ready for his and Quinn's approval early next week.

"Give me a call," said Manny. "We can decide then whether to meet here or at your showroom."

"That'll work."

Annabelle urged her to "Come back and see me soon, Chloe. And bring cookies."

Chloe promised that she would. She drove to the showroom, let Tai go home and got to work on the contract, planning out the estimated costs, room by room. At six, she closed up and headed for her house, a big, fat smile on her face and a thousand ideas for the redesign swirling in her brain.

She parked in her detached garage and was halfway along the short breezeway to the front door when she caught sight of the gorgeous bouquet of orchids and roses waiting in a clear, square vase on the porch. It must be from Quinn. The arrangement was so simple and lovely and the gesture so thoughtful, she let out a happy cry just at the sight of it.

Okay, it was a little silly to be so giddy at his thoughtfulness. But she hadn't had flowers in so long. Ted used to buy them for her, and since the divorce, well, she had no desire to buy them for herself. To her, a gorgeous bouquet of flowers just reminded her of Ted and all the ways she'd messed up her life. But if Quinn gave her flowers, she could start to see a beautiful arrangement in a whole new light.

She disarmed her alarm and unlocked the door—and then scooped up the vase and carried it in.

Dropping her purse on the entry bench, she took the vase straight to the kitchen peninsula, where she set it carefully down. The card had a red amaryllis on the front and the single word, Bloom. Bloom was the shop that belonged to Quinn's sister, Jody.

Whipping the little card off its plastic holder, she flipped it open and read *Beautiful flowers always remind me of you. I hate that it went so wrong for us. I miss you.*
    Ted

Chapter Four

"No!" Chloe shouted right out loud, not even caring that she sounded like some crazy person, yelling at thin air. "No, you do not get to do that. You do not." She tore the note in half and then in half again and she dropped it on the floor and stomped on it for good measure. They were *divorced*, for God's sake. He had a new wife. And all she wanted from him for now and forever was never to see or hear from him again.

Her heart racing with a sick kind of fury that he'd dared to encroach on her new life where he had no business being, Chloe whipped the beautiful flowers from the vase. Dripping water across the counter and onto the floor, too, she dropped them in the trash compactor, shoved it shut and turned the motor on. The compactor rumbled. She felt way too much satisfaction as the machine crushed the bright blooms to a pulp.

Once the flowers were toast, she poured the water

from the vase into the sink, whipped the compactor open again and dropped the vase on top of the mashed flowers. She ran the motor a second time, grinning like a madwoman when she heard that loud, scary pop that meant the vase was nothing but shards of broken glass. After that, she picked up the little bits of card, every one, threw them in with the shattered vase and the pulped flowers, took the plastic bag out of the compactor, lugged it out to the trash bin and threw it in.

Good riddance to bad trash.

She spent a while stewing, considering calling Ted and giving him a large piece of her mind.

But no. She wanted nothing to do with him and she certainly didn't want to make contact with him again. That might just encourage him.

She wondered if the flowers and the creepy note could be considered the act of a stalker.

But then she reminded herself that Ted and his bride, Larissa, lived more than a thousand miles away in San Diego. It was one thing for Ted to have his assistant send her flowers just to freak her out, but something else again for him to show up on her doorstep in person.

Wasn't going to happen. He was just being a jerk, an activity at which he excelled.

God. She had married him. How could she have been such an utter, complete fool?

Back in the house, she changed into jeans and a tank top. Then she took her time cooking an excellent dinner of fresh broiled trout with lemon butter, green beans and slivered almonds and her favorite salad of field greens, blueberries, Gorgonzola cheese and toasted walnuts, with a balsamic vinaigrette.

When it was ready, she set the table with her best dishes, lit a candle, poured herself a glass of really nice sauvignon blanc and sat down. She ate slowly, savoring every delicious bite.

A little later, she took a long scented bath and put on a comfy sleep shirt and shorts. Even after the bath, she was still buzzing with anger at the loser she'd once had the bad judgment to marry. Streaming a movie or reading a book was not going to settle her down. She needed a serious distraction.

So she went to the cozy room on the lower floor that she used as a home office and lost herself in the plans for Quinn's house. Within a few minutes of sitting down at her desk, the only thing on her mind was the rooms taking shape in her imagination—and on her sketch pad. And the numbers coming together for each room, for the project as a whole. She worked for hours and hardly noticed the time passing.

When she finally went back upstairs to the main floor, it was almost midnight. Time for bed.

But she didn't go to bed. It was cool out that evening. So she put on a big sweater over her sleep shirt, pulled on a pair of fluffy pink booties and went out onto her deck. It was something she had not done after dark since the night Quinn spent in her bed.

But she was doing it tonight.

She padded to the deck railing and stared down at Quinn's house.

Was she actually expecting him to be watching, waiting for the moment when she wandered out under the stars?

Not really. It just felt…reassuring somehow. To gaze down at his house, to know that she would see him again, would share dinner with him on Friday night.

When the French doors opened and he emerged, she let out a laugh of pure delight and waved to signal him up.

He didn't even hesitate, just went on down the steps at the side of his deck and forged up the hill. She went to meet him at the top of her stairs, feeling breathless and wonderful.

Tonight, he wore ripped old jeans, a white T-shirt that seemed to glow in the dark and the same moccasins he'd been wearing that other night. He said, "Love those furry boots." When she laughed, he added, "I was getting worried you might never come outside."

"And I was absolutely certain there was no way you might be glancing up to see if I was looking down for you." She held out her hand. He took it. His skin was warm, his palm callous. Just his touch made her body sing. "Come sit with me?"

He looked at her as though she were the only other person in the world. "Whatever you want, Chloe."

She tugged him over to the two chairs they'd sat in that other night and pulled him down beside her.

Silence.

But it was a good silence. They just sat there, staring out at the clear night and the distant mountains. A slight wind came up, rustling the nearby pines. And an owl hooted off in the shadows somewhere between his house and hers.

Finally, she said, "I met with Manny. I think it went well."

"He says so, too."

"And I'm in love with your daughter."

He chuckled, a rough and tempting sound. "She has that effect on people. Manny's tough, but Annabelle still manages to wrap him around her little finger. Truth is she rules the house. We just try to keep up with her."

She looked over at him. "Has she asked you about her mother again?"

"Not yet." He met her eyes through the shadows. "I

know, I know. Wait until she asks. And then don't load her up with more information than she's ready for."

"That's the way." She thought of the flowers she'd crushed in the compactor—and then pushed them out of her mind. Why ruin a lovely moment by bringing Ted into it?

Instead, she asked him how he had met Manny. He explained that the old ex-fighter had been his first professional trainer. "I met him at the first gym I walked into after leaving home. Downtown Gym, it was called, in Albuquerque. Manny ran the place and worked with the fighters who trained there. We got along. When I moved on, he went with me. I had a lot of trainers. And over time, Manny became more like my manager, I guess you could say. And kind of a cross between a best friend and a dad." He shot her a warning look. "But don't tell him I said that."

She grinned. "Why not?"

"He already thinks he knows what's best for me. If he ever heard I said I thought of him as a father, he'd never shut up with the advice and instructions."

She softly advised, "But I'll bet it would mean the world to him to know how you really feel."

"He knows. Hearing it out loud would only make him more impossible to live with." Quinn faked a dangerous scowl. "So keep your mouth shut."

She laughed and held up both hands. "I swear I'll never say a word."

"Good."

"So, how did he end up back here in Justice Creek with you and Annabelle?"

"I don't think either of us really considered a different option. He moved in with me when Annabelle was a baby, to help out."

When Annabelle was a baby...

So the little girl had been with her dad from the first? What had happened to the mother, the one Quinn said Annabelle would most likely never meet?

So many questions.

But Chloe had such a good feeling about the man beside her. She trusted him to tell her everything in his own good time.

He said, "When I decided to retire from the Octagon last year, Manny was already taking care of Annabelle full-time." Chloe knew what the Octagon was: the eight-sided ring in which Ultimate Fighting Championship mixed-martial-arts fighters competed. During the rough years when she was still married to Ted, she'd watched more than one of Quinn's televised UFC fights. It had lifted her spirits to see how far the wild, angry boy from her hometown had come. He continued, "I asked Manny to stick with me when I moved back home. He agreed right off, said he supposed it was about time he settled down. Annabelle's a handful, but so far he's managing."

"From what I've seen, he's great with her. He's patient, encourages her to express herself and make some of her own decisions—but he stays in charge, too."

"Yeah. He's a champ with her, all right..." Quinn's voice kind of trailed off and there was another silence, one somehow not as comfortable as the first.

She glanced over at him again and found him watching her. "Whatever it is, you might as well just say it."

"I got a question, but I don't want to freak you out."

An unpleasant shiver traveled down the backs of her arms and she thought of Ted again. Because if her freaking out could be involved, it probably had to do with Ted.

Then again, how would Quinn know that? She'd mentioned her ex once, on the night that Quinn came to her bed. What she'd told him had been far from flattering to Ted, but she'd said nothing about how thinking of him made her want to crush flowers and break expensive vases.

"Ask me," she said. "I can take it." The words came out sounding so confident. She was proud of them.

"All right, then. Does your mama know you're going out to dinner with me?"

Her mother. Of course. "No."

"It's Justice Creek, Chloe."

"Meaning she *will* know?"

"I'd say the odds are better than fifty-fifty, wouldn't you?"

Chloe kept her gaze steady on his. It was no hardship. Looking at him made her think of hot sex. And safety. And that combination really worked for her. "That girl—the mama's girl I was in high school?"

"Yeah?"

She slanted him a teasing glance. "You're not even going to argue that I was never a mama's girl?"

"Hey. You called it, not me."

And she made a low, rueful noise in her throat. "Yes, I did. And I was. But I'm not anymore. I tried living my life my mother's way. It didn't work for me. I'm all grown up now and my mother doesn't get to tell me what to do or whom to spend my time with."

One side of his beautiful mouth curved up then. It was a smirk, heavy on the irony, more like the old, dangerous, edgy Quinn from back in high school than the one she'd been getting to know lately. "*Whom*. Always so ladylike."

"Don't tease me. I'm serious."

His smirk vanished. "So you're admitting that your mother's not gonna like it, you and me spending time together?"

"What I'm telling you is that she doesn't have a say, so it doesn't matter whether she likes it or not."

He reached out his hand between their chairs. She put hers in it, and he lifted it to that wonderful mouth of his. Hot shivers cascaded down her arm and straight to the core of her, just at the feel of his soft lips against her skin. Then he rubbed his chin where his lips had been, teasing her with the rough brush of beard stubble, reminding her of their one night together, making her long to jump up and drag him inside.

But she didn't.

A moment later, he let go of her hand. He started talking again—about his plans for Prime Sports. She told him how much she appreciated the chance to rework the interiors at his house and then she shared with him some of the ideas she and Manny had discussed for upgrading the kitchen and opening up the living-room space.

A couple of hours passed as they sat there talking quietly under the waning moon. She even told him a little about her failed marriage—no, not about the flowers, and not about the times Ted had struck her. This thing with Quinn was so new and sweet and heady. Sharing ugly stories about her ex would definitely dim the romantic glow. Instead, she tried to explain how disappointed she was in the way things had turned out.

"It hurts so much," she confessed, "when something that should have been so right somehow goes all wrong. And I feel… I don't know, *less*, I guess. Shamed, that I didn't make better choices."

He regarded her for several seconds in that steady way he had. "You said the other night that the guy was abusive…"

She held his gaze as she shook her head.

He frowned. "I'll need more than a head shake to get what you're trying to tell me."

She let out a hard sigh. "Oh, Quinn. It's a beautiful night. And you're here beside me. It's good, you and me, talking like this."

"Yeah, it is."

"I probably shouldn't even have brought up my divorce."

"Yeah, you should. Whatever you want to tell me, that's what I want to hear."

"That's just it. I really don't want to go into any of that old garbage right now."

He gave her another of those long, thoughtful looks. And then, "All right."

And just like that, he let it go.

How amazing. He let it go. She'd grown up with a mother who never let anything go. And Ted? He would hound a person to hell and back to find out something he wanted to know.

But not Quinn. She said she didn't want to talk about it—and he just let it go. He said, "Whatever that story is, whatever happened in the past, you're going to be fine."

She made a low, rueful sound. "You're sure about that, huh?"

And he nodded. "You're brave and beautiful, Chloe— and not only on the outside. You're beautiful in your heart, where it matters. I admire the hell out of you."

Tears burned in her eyes at such praise. She blinked them away and whispered a soft, sincere "Thank you…"

By then, she really wanted to take him inside and spend a few more thrilling hours in his arms. But she felt somehow shyer now than that other night—shy and tentative.

And other than kissing her hand that one time, he'd made no move on her.

It was two in the morning when he said good-night.

She stood at the railing watching him jog down the hill to his house, and felt disappointed in herself that she'd let him go without so much as a single shared kiss.

But then, he *had* asked her out. She would see him again on Friday night...

Friday evening, Quinn arrived five minutes early. "Better grab a scarf," he warned.

She ran and got one, then followed him out across the breezeway and around the garage to the side parking space, where a gorgeous old convertible Buick coupe waited—top down, of course. With sidewalls so white they were blinding even in the shade.

"Wow." She couldn't resist gliding her palm over the glossy maroon paint. "It looks brand-new." The bright chrome gleamed in the fading early-evening light. It had round vents on the front fenders and an enormous, toothy grille.

"It's one of Carter's rebuilds. A '49 Buick Roadmaster." Carter, Quinn's oldest brother, designed and built custom cars. "I saw it at his shop a couple of weeks ago. Don't know what came over me, but I wanted it. So I bought it." He opened the door for her. She slid in onto the snow-white, tuck-and-roll bench seat. "Had him put seat belts in it, along with a decent sound system and power windows." He was leaning on the open door, bending close to her, his gray suit jacket already off and slung over his shoulder, hanging by a finger.

She got a hint of his aftershave, which was manly and fresh. He looked so good, in a white shirt and gray slacks, with a dark blue tie. She thought about kissing him, and turned away to run her hand over the leather seat in an effort to distract herself from a sudden, vivid memory of how pliant and hot his lips felt pressed to hers. "It's gorgeous," she said, altogether too breathlessly.

"Yeah." The single word seemed to dance along her nerve endings. She looked back up at him, and he grinned at her. And she just knew that *he* knew what she'd been thinking. "You look beautiful," he said, his gaze taking in her little black dress and her double strand of pearls that her dad had given her when she graduated from high school. "So smooth."

"Um, what?"

"You, Chloe. You're smooth."

"That's good, I hope?"

"That is excellent. Buckle up now." He shut the door as she tied her scarf over her hair.

He took her to the Sylvan Inn, which was a few miles southeast of town nestled in among the pines. The inn had a quiet atmosphere and great food.

"We used to come here when I was little," she said, once they were settled with their tall goblets of ice water, hot bread and giant menus in the traditional Sylvan Inn blue leather cover with the fancy gold lettering on the front. "For special occasions. My dad loves their hammer steaks. So do I, as a matter of fact."

"Good memories, then?"

"Very good." She glanced up at him—and spotted a familiar face across the dining room. Chloe smiled. The tall, thin blonde smiled right back. She gave Chloe a jaunty wave and disappeared behind a potted plant.

"What's up?" Quinn asked.

Chloe brushed a hand over the crisp white cuff of Quinn's shirt. "Don't look now, but we've been spotted by Monique Hightower. Did you know she works here?" They'd gone to school with Monique. The woman never met a secret she wouldn't share with the whole town.

"Uh-oh." He pretended to look worried. "Like I said the other night, it's Justice Creek. You go out with me, everyone in town is bound to know."

Now she brushed the back of his hand, which was warm and tan and dusted lightly with brown hair. It felt so good to touch him. She had to watch herself or she'd be all over the poor guy. "I hope you don't mind that the gossip mill will be churning."

"Me?" He gave a low chuckle. "I think I can deal with it."

"Such a brave man…"

They shared one of those looks. Long. Intimate. Wonderful. Finally, he said, "Read your menu, Chloe."

She closed the blue folder. "I did."

"You know what you want?"

"Oh, yes, I do." She said it slowly, with a lazy smile.

He warned low, "Keep looking at me like that and we won't make it through the appetizer."

But they did. They had it all. Appetizers, a nice bottle of cabernet, salad, hammer steaks with cheesy potatoes and a decadent chocolate dessert. And they took their sweet time about it.

Monique dropped by their table around nine, just after they'd been served their coffee and dessert. "Chloe. Quinn. What a surprise."

Quinn asked, "So, how's life treating you, Monique?"

"I'm getting by." Monique tossed her topknot of curly blond hair and stuck her hands in the pockets of her black service apron. "When did you two start spending time together?"

Chloe sipped her coffee. "This is our first date. I'm having a fabulous time."

Quinn said, "Chloe always had a thing for me, since way back in high school."

Monique blinked three times in rapid succession. "Really?"

Chloe stifled a silly giggle and said with great seriousness. "I finally got up the nerve to tell him." *And to show him, as a matter of fact.* "And then he asked me out. The rest could be history. I mean, if I play my cards right." She lowered her voice to a whisper. "But, Monique..."

Monique leaned a little closer. "What?"

"Don't say a word to anyone."

"Oh. Never. I would never tell a soul..." Translation: she couldn't wait to tell the world. Monique asked about Prime Sports, and Quinn gave her a card good for a free visit and one class of her choice. And then she turned to Chloe again, her dark eyes sharply gleaming. "I was so surprised when you moved back to town. I mean, we all knew you were headed for great things. No one ever would have guessed you'd end up running back home to Justice Creek. I'm just so *sorry* that things didn't work out for you."

Six months ago, Chloe would have been shamed and infuriated by Monique's barbed words and pretended concern. Or at the very least, embarrassed. At the moment, though, all she felt was amused. "Thanks, Monique. You're all heart."

Monique sighed heavily. Across the room, the manager who'd greeted them when they arrived had his eye on her. "Well, good to see you two. Gotta go." She scuttled off.

Chloe took a bite of her delicious dessert. "Everything we told her will be all over town. Twenty-four hours—thirty-six, max."

Quinn leaned closer and spoke low. "Maybe I shouldn't have said that you had a thing for me in high school."

She met his eyes directly and she couldn't keep from

grinning. "Are you kidding? I loved it. Not to mention it was the truth. If Monique Hightower's going to be spreading rumors about us, they might as well be true."

After their slow, wonderful meal, they returned to Chloe's house.

Quinn eased the gorgeous old car into the space beside the garage and turned off the engine. "Are you up for a walk around the block?"

"Sure." It was a nice night. "A walk would be great. We'll work off some of that amazing dessert."

He followed her inside and waited while she changed into flats. Then off they went, down the front steps and out to the street, where they strolled beneath the silver crescent of the moon.

Their development, Haltersham Heights, had no sidewalks. The houses were set back from the street, among the trees. Quinn stopped at a lot three doors down and across the street from Chloe's. It had a For Sale sign at the curb with a big SOLD plate stuck on it. The large contemporary log and natural stone house could be seen, windows gleaming, through the trees.

"The sold sign went up a few weeks ago," she said. "About time. This one's been on the market for months."

"I know. I bought it. Got a great price, too."

She laughed—and then she realized he wasn't kidding. "Wait a minute. You're serious?"

"I am." He put his hand over her fingers, where they curled around his arm. She'd barely had time to enjoy the flare of pleasure at how good his touch felt, when he said, "I bought it before I knew you would be fixing up my house. But it should work out great. We're closing on this one Monday, so we can move in here next week. We'll stay here while you renovate the other one—and not to get ahead of myself or anything, but once we move back to our house, you can start on this one. It's the same story as the other one. Solid construction, but it's begging to be brought into the twenty-first century. When you're finished, I'll sell it."

She only stared.

"Chloe, your mouth's hanging open."

"And why wouldn't it be? You're too much."

"Too much of what, exactly?"

"Well, let's see. Quinn Bravo, world-champion cage fighter, fitness empire builder, real estate mogul…"

"That all sounds pretty good to me."

"You must have made a fortune as a fighter, huh?"

"I did all right. The payout for winning a championship fight is a hefty one. And I landed some big-time endorsements, too."

"I think I'm speechless, Quinn."

He gave her his high school bad-boy smirk. "You'll get over it. And the truth is, Prime Sports will never make much money unless my franchise plan pays off. The housing market's rebounding nicely, though. I *can* make money in real estate."

She admitted softly, "Start-ups aren't easy, and I say that from experience. If you hire me for both of your houses, it will make a big difference for me. I really do need the business."

"So you've got it. Everybody wins."

She made a low, disbelieving sound. "As simple as that?"

His eyebrows drew together. "Why not?"

"I don't know. I wouldn't want to take advantage of you just because you, um, like me…"

He framed her face in his big, calloused hands. "Look at me."

"Oh, I am." She stared straight up into those soft aquamarine eyes and never wanted to look away. "I really am."

"Are you telling me you can't do the job?"

She stiffened and answered with heat, "Of course I can do the job."

He chuckled then. "See? We got no problem here."

Standing there in the darkness of her quiet street with his warm, rough hands cradling her cheeks, she decided he was right. "No, I guess we don't."

He lowered his head, until his sexy, plump lips were a hairbreadth from hers. He had lips like a girl's, but the rest of him was all man. "I got a request, though."

She longed for his kiss. Her heart was beating slow and deep. Sparks flared across her skin. And low in her belly, she seemed to be melting. "Oh, God. Anything."

"Work with my brother's company, Bravo Construction?"

She made herself focus on what he'd just asked of her—and it wasn't easy, with those lips of his so close.

Use his brother's company...

She'd left that possibility open-ended when she talked to Manny. But really, why not? Bravo Construction had a great reputation. She felt confident she could develop a solid working relationship with them. It could be good for everyone. "All right."

His warm breath touched her lips. The guy was driving her crazy. "I already talked to my sister Nell—just paving the way. Nell says she'll fit the project in the schedule and they can start work a week from Monday."

"That's quick."

"Yeah. And I like to keep it in the family if I can."

"I get that." She tried really hard not to sound as breathless as she felt. "No problem. Bravo Construction it is."

"Good, then."

"Quinn…"

"Hmm?" A teasing light shone in his eyes. She realized he knew exactly what he was doing to her.

And *she* knew that she couldn't take it anymore. She only had to lift herself up a fraction higher to get what she wanted. So she did. And it worked.

At last, he was kissing her.

"Chloe…" Quinn whispered her name right into her pretty mouth.

And then he let go of her arms—in order to pull her up nice and close. She tasted so good. Hot and wet.

And all of her, every graceful, sweetly scented inch of her, was so, so smooth.

Worth the endless, twelve-day wait since the last time he'd had his mouth on hers.

He lifted his head an inch. She let out a tiny moan, as though she couldn't bear not to have their mouths fused together. He slanted his head the other way and drank that moan right off her sweet, sweet lips.

Those slender arms glided up his chest and then her soft hands were stroking his collar, caressing his neck, her slim fingers threading up into the close-trimmed hair at the nape of his neck. He scraped his tongue along the smooth edges of her teeth, pushing deeper, into all that wet sweetness.

Coffee. Wine. Chocolate.

Chloe.

There had been women in his life, maybe too many. Especially when he was first making his name in the Octagon. Women liked fighters. And they particularly liked fighters who won. For a while there he'd gotten carried away with all the attention. Beautiful women everywhere he turned, his for the taking.

But even an endless chain of gorgeous women got old after a while. He started to see that to most of them, he was just a cheap thrill. And he wanted to be more than that to someone.

He found he wanted heart in a woman. He wanted someone he could talk to. He wanted real, gut-deep integrity. He wanted truth. He wanted a powerful connection.

Oh, and yeah. Brains and a sense of humor, too.

It wasn't that there weren't women out there with all that. It was just that most of them had no interest in a guy who still couldn't read past about fourth-grade level, a guy who got bloodied and battered for a living. Plus, when he was fighting, it ate up his life. He didn't have time to go looking for the one for him.

And then along came Annabelle. Her life, her happiness, her chance to grow up and take on the world—suddenly that was what mattered to him. To raise his little girl up right was more than enough. He didn't need that special woman, after all.

Or so he'd believed until twelve nights ago.

Until Chloe led him into her house and straight to her bed.

Chloe.

She had it all—everything he'd already accepted he wasn't going to find. And no one had ever tasted so good.

Reluctantly, he broke the kiss.

She stared up at him, eyes full of stars. "Come back to my house? Be with me tonight?"

"Damn, Chloe. I was afraid you'd never ask."

Her belly all aflutter with anticipation, her pulse a rushing sound in her ears and her cheeks feeling way hot-

ter than they should, Chloe ushered Quinn in her front
door and then turned to engage the lock and reset the
alarm. "You can hang your jacket there." She gestured
at the coatrack. He hung up his jacket, and she grabbed
his hand. "This way..."

But he held back, tugging her close, into the hard, hot
circle of his arms. He kissed her, a slow one that had her
knees going weak and a meltdown happening in her core.

However, when he lifted his head that time, his eyes
were way too serious.

She frowned, suddenly struck with concern for
whatever might be bothering him. "What is it? What's
wrong?"

He pulled her close again. And he whispered in her
ear, "I want to take all your clothes off and see you naked.
I want to kiss every inch of you."

She sighed. "We are definitely on the same page about
that."

"But..."

She pushed him away enough that she could see his
eyes. "Oh, no. There *is* something. What?"

"Don't look so worried." With his big thumb, he
smoothed the scrunched place between her eyebrows. "It's
nothing bad. I just have some things I want to say first."

Would she rather be kissing him? Absolutely. But then
again, whatever he wanted to say, she wanted to hear.
"So...coffee or something?"

"Sure."

She led him into the kitchen and whipped him up a
quick cup, pouring cream in a little pitcher because she'd
watched him at dinner and knew he took cream.

"Aren't you having any?" he asked.

Her tummy was all fluttery, what with wondering
what kind of thing he just *had* to say to her. Coffee would

only make it worse. "Maybe later. How about the living area? It's more comfortable there."

"Good enough." He poured in the cream, picked up his cup and followed her to the sofa.

They sat down together, and he set his cup on the coffee table. She folded her hands tightly in her lap. He'd said it was nothing awful, but he seemed so intense suddenly…

Was there going to be drama? Oh, she hoped not. She'd had enough drama to last her a lifetime, and then some.

He said, "There are things about me I want you to know."

Uh-oh. She gulped down the giant lump in her throat and gave him a nod to continue.

"First, about Annabelle's mother."

Chloe realized she'd been holding her breath. She let it out slowly. Annabelle's mother. Actually, she really wanted to know about Annabelle's mother…

"Her name is Sandrine Cox. She's an actress and model. We went out a few times. She got pregnant. She came to me, told me she was fairly certain it was my baby and she felt I had a right to know."

Chloe studied his wonderful face. He seemed… relaxed when he talked about his little girl's mother. Relaxed and accepting. "You believed her."

"Yeah. Sandrine was always straight ahead about things. I believed that *she* believed the baby was mine. Then later, right after Annabelle was born, a paternity test proved Sandrine was right. Annabelle's mine. And I knew from the moment Sandrine told me she was pregnant that I wanted the baby. Sandrine didn't. She didn't want to be a mom. She liked her single life and she had a lot of ambition, a heavy focus on her career. I made her an offer. I would pay her a large lump sum to have the baby and then she would sign over all rights to me."

"And that's what happened?"

He nodded. "She kept her end of the bargain. I kept mine."

"You haven't heard from her since Annabelle was born?"

"No. I doubt I ever will."

"But with something as important as a child, Quinn, you never know. Someday Annabelle's mother might regret her choice, change her mind."

"Anything's possible."

"And if she did come to you, if she wanted to meet Annabelle?"

"Can't say for certain. If she was as honest and upfront as before, we would work something out so that she could know Annabelle and Annabelle could know her."

Chloe liked his answer. It could be difficult for him to make room for his daughter's mother in their lives. But it was the right thing. "That sounds good. For Annabelle, most of all. It's very likely, as she grows to adulthood, that she's going to want to know about her birth mother and meet her, if possible."

"Maybe. But it's like you told me that first night. I'm not going to borrow trouble. I'll answer Annabelle's questions and pay attention to the signals she gives me. And then take it from there." He loosened his tie. "I didn't want you to wonder anymore about how I ended up with sole custody of my little girl and no mother in sight."

Tenderness washed through her—for him, for the kind of man he was. A good man. Honest. True-hearted. A man who would do what was right even if it wasn't the best or easiest thing for him, personally.

She reached out and brushed his hand. "Let me..."

He sat so still, so watchful, as she undid the tie completely. It made a soft, slithering sound as she slipped it from around his neck. She laid it carefully over the arm of the sofa. Then she turned to him again and unbuttoned the top two buttons of his snowy dress shirt, smoothing the collar open, revealing the powerful column of his neck and the sharp black point of one of those intricate tattoos that covered his shoulder and twined halfway down his arm.

"Better?" she asked.

They shared a smile as he nodded. He said, "There's more."

She took his right hand and turned it over, revealing his cuff buttons. One by one, she undid them. "Tell me."

"I'm dyslexic," he said, his voice rougher than usual, freighted with something wary, something wounded. "You know what dyslexia is?"

"I think I do. I think I remember reading that it's when a person has difficulty in learning to read or interpret words, letters and other symbols?"

"That's pretty close to the generally accepted definition."

She took his left hand and unbuttoned that cuff, too.

He spoke again. "Most people think dyslexia is what you just said. A learning disorder, period. It's more. It's a challenge, a tough one. But it's a gift, too." She sat with his hand in her lap, the buttons undone, drinking in every word, as he explained, "You remember how I was as a kid. Trouble. Always getting in fights. Everyone thought I was stupid because I couldn't get the hang of reading. I hated school, hated being the slow kid. I acted out constantly. Only later did I figure out that my problem was I couldn't learn the way most kids learn. A traditional school environment did nothing for me. I don't get phonics, don't get learning things in rote sequence. It completely overloads me. So I would lash out."

She did remember that troubled boy so well. "You always seemed so angry."

"You bet I was. By the time I was eleven, my mother was at the end of her rope with me. As a last-ditch effort to find something I could do well, she enrolled me in a karate class—and everything changed for me. For once, I got something, really *got* it. Yeah, I have to work my ass off to try and get the meaning out of a line of letters across a page. But I'd always been damn good at fighting. The way my brain is wired makes me more capable than most people of visualizing the moves of my opponents in advance. I see the whole picture, I guess you could say. And that makes me more willing to follow my instincts. So I was good at karate, and finally being good at something was damn motivating. It got me going, gave me hope. I was driven to excel." He took her hand then and wove his fingers with hers.

It felt so good, her hand in his. She held on tight. "Answer me a question…"

"Name it."

"You seemed nervous about telling me this. Were you?"

He squeezed her fingers. "Yeah, I was."

"But I can't see why you would be, not after the way your life's worked out."

"There's more. And you need to hear it."

She *needed* to hear it? She almost asked him why, but then decided that the whys could wait. "All right…"

"Dyslexia is often genetic."

She frowned. "So you're telling me that Annabelle is dyslexic?"

"No. So far, Annabelle shows none of the signs. Already, she can recognize her alphabet and sound out simple words. But you should know that any child of mine could possibly be dyslexic."

She should know? It was an odd way to phrase it.

And he still had more to say. "I plan to be proactive. If a kid of mine showed signs of dyslexia, I would be on it, arranging for early testing, providing alternative learning systems and support, working with the school so everyone's on the same page about what needs to be done. If one of my kids was dyslexic, I would see to it that he didn't have to go through the crap I went through. I would make sure any kid of mine never had to feel stupid and incompetent and lag way behind the learning curve." He tipped his head then and asked with wry good humor, "You still with me, Chloe?"

"Absolutely. Yes. And I'm so sorry, Quinn. That you felt stupid and incompetent when you were little. No child should have to feel that way."

"I got past it."

"That doesn't make it right." At his chuckle, she chided, "It's nothing to joke about, Quinn."

He shrugged. "Tell me something."

She had that odd feeling again; there was more going on here than she was picking up. "Of course."

He let go of her hand, reached for his coffee—and said just what she'd been thinking. "Do you have any clue why I'm laying all this on you?"

She watched him take a sip. "Whatever your reasons, I have to say it's really nice to have a guy just sit right down and talk to me about the toughest things. It's rare."

"Right." He set the cup down again and rolled one of his unbuttoned cuffs to the elbow. "It's what women love. A guy who won't shut up…"

"I don't know about 'women.' But I know what *I* like.

And you telling me about what matters to you, about what made you who you are? I do like that. A lot."

"Well, all right." He rolled the other cuff. She watched him, admiring the hard shape of his arms, thick with muscle, roped with tendons, dusted with light brown hair, nicked here and there with small white ridges of scar tissue. He went on, "But I do have a reason for loading you up with way more info than you asked for."

"And I keep trying to make you see that you don't *need* a reason."

He slanted her a teasing look. "Got that."

A low laugh escaped her. "Well, okay, then. I get it. You're trying to tell me the reason—so go ahead. I'm ready for it."

"You sure?"

She groaned and executed a major eye roll. "Will you *please* stop teasing me?"

Now he looked at her so steadily, a look that made her warm all over, especially down in the center of her. "All right." And then, just like that, he said, "I want to marry you, Chloe."

Chapter Five

Quinn wasn't finished. "I want to build a life with you, have kids with you. Like I said, I'm a guy who follows my intuition, a guy who has trouble sounding out a word—but also a guy who gets the big picture. And once I know what I want, I go for it. I want you, Chloe, for my wife. I want you for my little girl, too, because I know you'll be the mother Annabelle needs."

Chloe just stared at him. Words? They'd completely deserted her.

He put up a hand. "It's okay. You don't have to say anything now. All you have to do is take your time. Think it over. And you should know the kids aren't a deal breaker for me. I want more. But if you don't, I can live with that. Annabelle will be enough."

"I, um…" She had no idea what to say next.

That didn't seem to bother him. He simply waited.

And she found that she couldn't sit still. She got up,

eased from behind the coffee table and then kept going to the sliding door, the one she'd slipped out that first night, when he came up the hill and she took him to her bed.

He didn't try to stop her. He didn't say a word, only sat there, patiently waiting for her to process all he'd just said.

She appreciated his silence and stillness now, appreciated it every bit as much as she did all that he'd told her moments before. She flipped on the deck lights and stared out at the two empty cedar chairs.

Was this really happening? Just like that, out of nowhere, he wanted to marry her?

But then again, no. Not out of nowhere, not really. He was such a focused sort of man. Of course, he would decide what he wanted and lay it all out for her so honestly and directly.

She fiddled with the pearls her dad had given her years ago, when she thought she knew everything and saw so clearly how her life would go.

What about love? Quinn hadn't mentioned love.

Should that bother her?

Well, it didn't. She'd had enough declarations of love from her rotten-hearted ex-husband to last her into the next century. And where had all that love talk gotten her but wounded, divorced and bitterly disappointed?

This, what Quinn offered, was better.

It wasn't a fantasy, not perfect. But it was honest. It felt real.

Quinn spoke then. "One more thing. About Manny…" He waited for her to look at him, and then for acknowledgement that she'd heard what he said. When she gulped and nodded, he went on. "Manny's part of the family. So you would not only be getting me and Annabelle. There's Manny, too. He can be a pain in the ass, I know. But he's not going anywhere. If you said yes, you would need to deal with him, work with him."

She felt a soft smile tremble across her mouth. "I would never for a second expect it to be any other way."

He didn't smile. But his eyes were so bright. "Well, all right, then."

The part about Manny had been so easy to answer. But the rest of it… She really didn't know what to say. She stared out the sliding door again.

He asked into the heavy silence, "Want me to go?"

Turning from her study of the empty deck chairs, she faced him once more. "No way. I want you to stay."

He stood. "Will you think about it, consider my offer?"

"I will."

He came for her then. She waited, her whole body humming with sweet anticipation as he approached.

And when he was close enough that the heat he generated seemed to reach out and touch her, she canted her chin higher and gazed straight into those beautiful eyes. "You are like no one I've ever known."

"That's good, I hope?"

"Oh, yes. It's very good."

"Angel." He lifted a big hand and brushed a finger down the curve of her cheek, stirring up goose bumps, making her sigh. And then he lowered that wonderful mouth of his and brushed those lips, so gently, back and forth across her own.

She smiled into his kiss, brought her hands up between them and went to work undoing the rest of the buttons down the front of his shirt. It didn't take long. She spread the shirt wide and pressed her palms to his broad chest, to that beautiful tattoo with his little girl's name in the middle of it. His skin was hot, wonderfully so. Sandy hair formed a tempting T across.

And down.

Best of all, she could count the strong beats of his big heart. She whispered against those velvety lips of his, "I should have made a move on you back in high school."

He chuckled, the low rumble sending a thrill shivering straight to the core of her. "That wasn't your style— and I wasn't your type."

"Oh, but Quinn. You *were* my type. What a fool I was then. I took what I thought was the safe way—and it wasn't safe in the least. It turned out all wrong."

"Hey." His voice was heaven, the perfect blend of rough and tender. He kissed the tip of her nose. "No regrets, huh?"

"But I do have regrets." She slid her hands up over his thick, hard shoulders, and clasped them around his neck. "And I can't just wish them away."

He shrugged out of his shirt and let it fall. Then he bent his head lower, smoothed her hair aside and pressed his hot mouth to the crook of her neck. "Forget 'em, then." His breath so hot across her skin, branding her, burning her. "For now, at least?"

She threaded her eager fingers up into his hair. "Help me with that?"

"Happy to." He breathed in through his nose. "You smell so good…" And then he scraped his teeth where his lips had been.

She shivered and moaned as he kissed his way back up over the curve of her jaw to claim her lips again. She opened for him. Heat speared through her as his tongue swept her mouth.

He lifted her hair off her neck with one hand. With the other, he took down the long zipper at the back of her dress and guided the dress off her shoulders. It dropped to the floor. She broke the lovely kiss in order to step out of it. He bent, picked it up and tossed it on the nearest chair.

Unbuttoning and unzipping, flinging articles of clothing toward the chair as soon as they had them off, they undressed each other.

Finally, when the only thing left was her pearls, he ordered gruffly, "Turn around."

She showed him her back. He unhooked the diamond clasp and took the necklace away. She faced him again in time to watch him reach over and lay the double strand on the nearby side table.

That was it. They were naked. Completely naked. And it seemed such a very long way to the bedroom.

Good thing she'd planned ahead.

He asked roughly, "What are you smiling about?"

And she pulled open the little drawer in the side table and took out the condom she'd tucked in there. Just in case.

"God. Chloe." He hauled her close, licked her ear and whispered in it, "You think of everything."

She whispered back, "A design teacher I had once told me that what I lack in imagination, I make up for in efficiency and good planning. I was really insulted at the time."

He took her earlobe between his teeth and tugged on it, biting down just a little harder than he needed to.

It felt so good it made her moan.

He whispered, "Put it on me."

She pulled back a little, far enough to meet his eyes. They were the color of some tropical sea right then, so deep, going down and down to deeper blue. Focused so completely on her. "Right now?"

For that she got a slow, deliberate nod from him.

She started to tear the top off the pouch.

"On second thought…" He caught her hand. "Wait…" And he pulled her close and kissed her some more. She gave herself up to that, to the taste of his mouth and the heat of his breath, to the feel of him, fully erect against her belly, making her burn for him.

Making her moan. She eased her free hand between them and wrapped her fingers around him, stroking. Oh, he felt so good—his powerful body pressed close, his mouth covering hers, the long, hard length of him held tight in her grip.

He kissed her endlessly, kissed her and caressed her, his fingers tracing magical patterns over her skin, teasing her breasts, first cradling them so gently, then catching the nipples, rolling them, so that she moaned some more. He seemed to really like it when she moaned.

He made a wonderful growling sound low in his throat. "Yeah," he said. "Like that?"

She couldn't say "Yes" fast enough. So she said it again, moving her hand up and down the thick length of him. "Yes…" And again, "Oh, yes, Quinn. Like that…"

And then his hand went lower, all the way to the feminine heart of her.

She cried out as he stroked her, opening her. She felt her own wetness, her readiness for him. She didn't want to wait a second longer. She couldn't wait…

"I…" She got that word out, and then couldn't for the life of her remember what she'd meant to say next.

"Yeah?" He was kissing his way along the line of her jaw, biting a little, licking some, too. Below, his fingers kept up their clever, thrilling play on her wet, secret flesh.

Oh, she was lost in the best way, totally gone. She kept her left hand wrapped around him, holding on for dear life. In her right, she still clutched the unused condom. She kind of waved it at him. "I…" Just that word. Nothing more. It was the only word she seemed to have at her disposal at the moment.

And apparently it was enough. He took the condom from her. She opened her eyes and stared up at him, dazed. Transported.

He lifted the small pouch, caught the corner between his teeth and tore the top off, all the while staring directly into her eyes, his other hand continuing to do amazing things to her below.

"Here," she whispered, holding out her free hand. He gave it back. She let go of him to use both hands, removing the wrapper and dropping it on the little table next to her pearls. And then she rolled the protection down over him. He moaned. And she granted him a small, triumphant smile. "There."

He reached for her, clasping her waist. She gasped in surprise. His right hand was slick and wet. It was *her* wetness, her desire. She was shocked at herself, at her own complete abandon.

Shocked. Amazed.

And gratified.

It was the same as that other night. Only better. He took her, claimed her, carried her right out of herself. He just swept her away—at the same time as he made her feel that she'd somehow come home, that nothing and no one would ever hurt her again.

And then he was lifting her. He did it so effortlessly, as though she weighed nothing. She grabbed for him, hungry for the feel of him, for her flesh pressed to his flesh, hot and tight and hard. She wrapped her arms and legs around him.

He whispered her name.

"Quinn," she whispered in return. "Oh, yes." She sank her teeth into his neck and when he growled at her, a dark, hot laugh escaped her. He bent to nuzzle her and she turned her face to his and claimed his mouth.

The kiss went deeper, wetter, hotter. And he was moving, with her all twined around him like a vine. He went to the short section of bare wall beside the entry closet, just walked her right up to it.

And then he lifted her, positioning her just so...

She felt him there, nudging her, right where she wanted him. And she pressed down.

He made the deepest, hottest, hungriest sound then, as she lowered herself onto him. He was wonderfully thick and large. Still, her body took him easily, gliding down around him until he filled her all the way.

They froze. She let her head fall back and her eyes drift shut. He had her perfectly braced, with the wall to give them stability. He canted his upper body slightly away from her, while below, he held her so close, just right, big hands cradling her open thighs. She clutched his shoulders, fingers gripping tight, her legs locked securely behind his waist.

She was...gone, lost in wonder, swept up in the connection, her breathing harsh and hungry, just like his.

"Chloe..."

And she opened her eyes and looked at him. His blue-green gaze was right there, waiting for her. He gripped her thighs tighter, pushing them wider, pressing his lower body closer, sliding into her that fraction deeper.

That did it. She felt the gathering, the build—and the lovely, hot sensation, as though all of her was blooming.

She asked, "Quinn?" For permission? Acknowledgment?

She had no idea which.

But he seemed to understand, even if she didn't. "Yeah,"

he answered, one corner of that soft, bad boy's mouth of his curling upward. "Go for it, angel."

And she did. She let go, let it happen, let it roll out from her in a hot, endless wave. Pleasure cascaded from the core of her, sizzling along every nerve, hitting the tips of her toes and the top of her head, spilling all through her in a flood of light and glory. He stayed with her, pressing up into her hard and tight, as the fire flamed so bright and then slowly faded down to a lovely, glowing ember.

And right then, when she thought it was over, when she was more than ready to ease her shaking legs to the floor, he started to move again.

She groaned in sexual overload and shoved fitfully at his rocklike shoulders. But he didn't release her.

And, well, could she blame him? After all, it *was* his turn. He'd swept her right off her feet and straight to paradise. The least she could do was stick with him now.

With a sigh of surrender, she stopped pushing him away and held on instead, bracing to ride it out.

But then, out of nowhere, all at once, it became more than just sticking with it for his sake. So much more.

In a split second, she was catching fire again.

"Oh… Oh, my!" She yanked him tight against her.

He let out a laugh, deep and knowing. Full of heat and joy.

She moaned his name as she pressed her open mouth to his, her body moving in time with his, picking up speed, finding the hard, insistent rhythm he set—and matching it, giving it back to him.

Time whirled away. The edge of the world was waiting for her. Waiting for both of them. She spun toward it, dizzy with the thrill of it. She hovered on the brink—and went over.

And he was right there with her, hitting the peak a moment after she did, pulsing hard and hot within her.

And then following her down.

Chapter Six

It was three-fifteen on Saturday morning when he left her.

Chloe put on a robe and walked him out to his beautiful old car. She kissed him goodbye—a long, slow, lovely kiss.

When he would have let her go, she grabbed him back and kissed him some more.

He laughed when he finally lifted his head. "Hey. I'm only going around the block."

"I know." She sighed, wrapped her arms around his waist, and beamed up at him. "But I want to make sure you don't forget me."

"No chance of that." He took a curl of her hair and wrapped it around his hand. "We got a special thing going, you and me."

"Oh, yes, we do."

He touched her chin with his thumb, brushed one last kiss across her upturned lips. "Get some rest."

She promised she would and reluctantly stepped back so he could open the car door and slide in behind the wheel. Then she waited, her arms wrapped around herself against the predawn chill, as he backed from the driveway and drove off down the street.

As soon as his taillights disappeared, she missed him. She wanted to run inside, grab the phone and call him back.

Which was totally silly. He'd asked her to marry him. And she was redecorating his house—*both* of his houses, as a matter of fact.

One way or another, she would be seeing him very soon.

She saw him the next day. He called and invited her out for ice cream with him and Annabelle. Chloe spent two lovely hours with father and daughter. Annabelle enchanted her. It might be too soon to talk about falling in love with Quinn. But she had no problem admitting she was head over heels for his little girl.

And then, that night, Quinn came up the hill to join her. He stayed for two hours. They talked about Annabelle and about Chloe's plans for his houses—and then they made love. He left at a little past midnight.

Same thing on Sunday night.

Monday at nine in the morning, Quinn closed on the house across the street from Chloe. Then, at eleven, he brought Manny and Annabelle to Chloe's showroom to see the plans and sign the contract for the redesign of the house down the hill. Chloe had cookies on offer at the coffee table, which Annabelle spotted immediately. Manny said she could have one.

Annabelle chose a cookie, thanked Chloe sweetly—

and asked if she knew how to make a fairy princess dress. "I want one, Chloe. Will you *please* make me one?"

Before Chloe could reply that she absolutely could and would, Quinn said, "Anniefannie, you are pushing it."

"Daddy!" The little girl tipped her cute nose high in a perfect imitation of disdain. "I'm not a fannie."

"But will you stop pushing it?"

Annabelle dimpled adorably. "But Chloe can make a *room*. I know she can make me a fairy princess dress." She turned pleading eyes on Chloe, who longed only to give her whatever she wanted. "Pleeeaaase, Chloe."

Manny spoke up then. He said one word. "Annabelle." After which he pushed back his chair and held out his hand.

Annabelle's lower lip started quivering. "Oh, no. Not the *car*. I don't want to sit in the *car*. Pleeaaassse, Manny."

Manny let out a heavy sigh. "Are you gonna stop pestering Chloe and sit quietly at the table while we finish our business here?"

Annabelle announced loudly, "Yes, I am!"

Manny mimed locking his lips with a key.

Annabelle straightened her small shoulders and folded her hands on the table, all the while pressing her lips together and pointedly glancing from one adult to the next.

Finally, Manny nodded. "All right. We'll give it a try."

Annabelle nodded wildly but kept her little mouth tightly shut.

"Eat your cookie," Quinn said in his gentlest voice.

Annabelle made short work of the treat. And then Manny gave her a cup of crayons and some paper. She was a perfect little angel, happily coloring away as the grown-ups finished their meeting.

That afternoon, Chloe visited Bravo Construction, which consisted of three trailers and a warehouse on the southwest edge of town. She met with Nell Bravo, who was in her late twenties and stunningly beautiful, with long auburn hair and a vivid half-sleeve tattoo down her shapely left arm. The baby of the Bravo family, Nell had always been outspoken and tough-minded. Everyone knew you didn't mess with Nell.

Chloe had the plans with her for Quinn's redesign. She spent two hours in Nell's office trailer, going over everything in detail, coming to agreement on the budget and the schedule.

Nell would personally run the job. Tomorrow, Chloe would get busy ordering cabinets and appliances, counters and flooring. Nell would put in for the permits they would need. Demo would begin first thing next Monday morning. If all went as planned—which it rarely did— the project would take nine to ten weeks.

At four o'clock, when they had everything pretty well hammered out, Chloe got up to leave.

And Nell hoisted her heavy black biker boots up onto her battered desk. "Before you head out, we need to talk. Hey, Ruby?"

The plump, motherly looking clerk at the desk near the door glanced around. "What do you need?"

"Take fifteen?"

"Sure." Ruby got up from her laptop and left the trailer.

Chloe had a sinking feeling in her stomach.

Nell proved the feeling right as soon as the door closed behind the clerk. "So, I hear you've had a thing for Quinn ever since high school. Is that true?"

Chloe dropped back into her chair. "Monique Hightower's been talking."

"Did you think she wouldn't?"

Chloe suppressed a sigh. "No. I knew she would." It had all seemed so amusing Friday night. But looking in

Nell's narrowed eyes right now, she didn't think it was funny at all.

Quinn's sister demanded, "Answer my first question."

Chloe drew herself up. "Yeah. I had certain...fantasies about Quinn way back when. Is that somehow a crime?"

"He's not just a piece of tasty meat. He's a good man."

Tasty meat? Chloe took care to keep her voice even. "I know he's a good man, Nell."

"You slumming?"

Chloe didn't let her gaze waver. "I absolutely am not— and why would you think that? Quinn's a brilliant man with a whole lot going for him. The word *slumming* just doesn't apply."

"Oh, come on, Chloe. Your mother was practically best friends with my father's first wife. No way Linda Winchester's going to approve of you seeing one of the bastard Bravos—especially not the 'stupid' one who barely managed to finish high school."

Chloe felt the angry color flooding upward on her cheeks. When would people stop assuming that her mother made her choices for her? "Nell." She made a show of clucking her tongue. "Where do I even start with you? Not fair. Not to Quinn. And not to me. He's far from stupid and he's done just fine for himself. We both know that. As for me, yes, it's true. I *used* to let my mother have way too much influence over me. But that was then. Right this minute, I'm thirty-one, divorced, fully self-supporting and on my own. My mother has zero say about whom I go out with."

Nell's lush mouth twisted. "Does your mother know that?"

Busted. "I'll say it again. *I* decide whom I spend time with."

Nell dropped her heavy boots to the floor, braced both

elbows on the desk and folded her hands between them. "Am I pissing you off, Chloe?"

The perennial good girl in Chloe pushed for denial, for smoothing things over after neatly sweeping them under the carpet. But no. The truth was better. "Yes, Nell. You are pissing me off."

"Good." Nell tipped her head to the side. The overhead fluorescents made her fabulous hair shimmer like a red waterfall. "Don't you hurt him, or you'll be answering to me."

Chloe sat tall. "I don't know for sure what's going to happen. But Quinn's an amazing man who means a lot to me. The last thing I would ever want to do is hurt him."

Nell's swivel chair squeaked as she flopped back in it and folded her arms across her spectacular breasts. She stared at Chloe, unblinking, for a grim count of ten. Then: "Look. I like your plans for the house. You know your job. I like the way you carry yourself. And I hardly knew you, back in the day. You were four years ahead of me in school. I only knew your reputation as the perfect one, the one headed for a good marriage to a rich husband, two-point-two children, a soccer-mom-and-country-club life—and some chichi career that you could fit in between social engagements."

"Something like interior design, you mean?"

"Hey. If the glass slipper fits…"

"As it turned out, it didn't. Not by a long shot. And that was then, Nell. I'm not that girl anymore."

Another long, measuring stare from Nell. Finally, she shrugged. "You know, I think I believe you." She got up and held down her hand. Chloe did want peace with Quinn's sister—with all of his family. After a moment's hesitation, she took Nell's offered hand and rose. Nell said, "Looking forward to working with you."

"I'm sure it will be interesting."

"Right. And listen. When you tell Quinn about this little talk we had—"

Chloe didn't even let her finish. "Why would I tell him? The way I see it, what just happened is between you and me."

Nell arched an auburn eyebrow. "Fair enough." And then she grumbled, "I'm really starting to like you. How 'bout that?"

"I'm glad. I'm going to do my best not to disappoint you—though you did go a little overboard just now."

Always a fighter, Nell stuck out her chin. "You think so?"

"Yes, I do. Then again, it's nice to know how much you love your brother and that you have his back."

That evening, Chloe spent a pleasant hour with a sketch pad, drawing a series of small figures that looked a lot like Annabelle. The figures all wore different versions of a magical, multilayered, brightly colored fairy princess costume, complete with wings—because what's a fairy princess costume unless there are wings?

A little later, when Quinn showed up, she took him downstairs to her home office and showed him the drawings.

"She would love it," he admitted with some reluctance. And then he shook his head. "You know she wants a puppy, too? There's no end to what Annabelle wants."

Chloe laughed. "The puppy's your problem."

"So far, we're holding the line on that."

"I just want to make this costume for her."

He took the sketch pad from her, dropped it to her desk, then wrapped his arms around her and kissed the end of her nose. "You're a pushover."

She grinned up at him. "I promise to get myself under

control soon when it comes to dealing with her. But I want to do this for her. I want her to have her dream room and I want her to have her fairy princess dress."

He chuckled. "You're giving me the big eyes. You're as bad as she is."

She traced the crew neck of his Prime Sports T-shirt with her index finger and then she pressed her lips against the hot skin of his powerful neck. "I would need to take her measurements, and probably let her see the sketches, to make sure I've got it right, got it just as she imagines it. So she would have to know ahead of time that she was getting what she wanted…"

"Yep. The big eyes," he muttered gruffly. "I know what you're doing." He kissed her then, a lovely, deep, slow one, after which she sighed and gazed up at him hopefully. Finally, he grumbled, "Wait a week or two before you bring it up to her. At least she won't think all she has to do is bat her eyes and beg a little and everything she wants will just drop in her lap."

"I'll check with Manny, too, to make sure he's okay with it. And if he gives the go-ahead, I'll wait two weeks to show her the drawings. How's that?" she asked, batting her eyes for all she was worth.

He gave in. "Fine."

"Thanks." She sighed and turned in his embrace so she could lean back against him.

He put his arms around her waist, and she felt his warm lips in her hair. "How'd your meeting with Nell go?"

Chloe thought of his little sister's biker boots hitting the desk, of the hot, protective gleam in Nell's emerald-green eyes. "Great. I like her. I think we'll work well together."

"She can be a hard ass. Don't let her intimidate you."

Chloe smiled to herself. "Not a chance."

And then she caught his hand and led him back upstairs to her bedroom, where they made slow, delicious love.

He put his clothes back on at a little after midnight. She hated to see him go and she told him so. And then she kind of waited for him to point out that, if they were married, he wouldn't have to go.

But then he just kissed her again and said he'd see her tomorrow.

She put on her robe and walked him to the sliding door in the great room. Once he was gone, she stood looking out at the stars, thinking about saying yes to him.

Wanting to.

Because she wanted *him*. She *liked* him—and she liked his daughter and Manny, too. He wanted a wife and a mother for Annabelle. And all her life, she'd longed to be an excellent wife to a good and decent man, to be a loving mother. The idea of having Annabelle as her own made her heart feel too big for her chest. And the part about having Quinn's babies?

That hollowed her out and made her burn.

But speaking of burning…she'd been burned before, and badly. And it hadn't even been three weeks since that first night Quinn came up the hill and joined her in her bed.

How could she be sure of him in such a short time? With her track record, how could she be sure of anyone?

The stars outside were silent. They had no answers for her.

Tuesday flew by. She had several customers at the showroom. And she had shopping to do, an endless list of goodies that would be needed for Quinn's remodel.

When Chloe got home that evening, she saw a moving van at the house across the street. She went on over. Manny was there, directing the movers. He greeted her with a grin and a hug and said that Quinn was down at the other house feeding Annabelle her dinner on the last night they would spend at home until after the re-modeling.

Chloe explained about the fairy princess dress.

Manny said, "She's gonna love that."

"So it's okay with you? You don't think I'm a com-plete pushover?"

"I think we got a little girl who loves her princesses. And you want to help her with that. Sounds about right to me."

She thanked him and then glanced around, admir-ing the soaring stone fireplace and the thick log walls. "Give me a tour?"

"Getting ideas for this one already?"

She nodded. "I'm happy that I'll have a chance to get to know this house ahead of time, get familiar with it, you know? I'll have an opportunity to mull over what changes will work best for it. Redoing a log home pres-ents a special set of challenges."

Manny seemed to be studying her. "You're all right, Chloe."

"I'm glad you think so, Manny. I'm growing quite fond of you, as well."

"Quinn pop the question yet?"

Chloe fell back a step. "He told you he was going to?"

"Hell, no. He told me zip. But we been together more than a decade. I got a good idea what's going on with him, whether he lays it out for me or not." The two burly moving guys came in with the dining-room table. Manny said, "Through there, boys." And on they went. Manny lowered his voice for Chloe alone and said, "You haven't said yes yet, have you?"

Chloe pretended to ponder. "Hmm. Let me see. Would Quinn really want me to answer that?"

Manny chortled out a rough laugh. "Come on. Let me show you the house…"

The landline was ringing when Chloe got back to her place. It clicked over to her old-school answering machine before she could pick up.

It was her mother. "Sweetheart, we're home. Walked in the door five minutes ago. Maui was heaven, as always. But it's nice to be back and I can't want to see you, find out how you've been doing and tell you all about our trip. Call me the minute you get this. Love you…"

Chloe stood by the phone and considered getting it over with, calling her mother back right away. Years of conditioning had her feeling she really *ought* to call now, that a good daughter could be counted on to keep in contact with the ones she loved.

But as soon as her mother asked her what she'd been up to in the past two weeks, Chloe would be confronted with the question of how much to say.

Ha. As if there was a choice. Monique Hightower was spreading the news about her and Quinn far and wide. One way or another, it wouldn't be long before her mother got an earful. And it would probably be better if her mother heard it from Chloe.

Better being a relative term, knowing her mother.

Chloe picked up the phone.

And then set it back down again.

Her hand was shaking slightly, and that made her mad. Why should she live in fear of her own mother? She'd faced Nell Bravo right down and told her that Linda Winchester did not run her life. She'd told Quinn the same thing. She needed to live by her own words.

Chloe turned the ringer off on the kitchen and bedroom phones and turned the volume on the message machine all the way down. Then she switched the sound off on her cell, as well. She'd check to see who'd called her at *her* convenience, thank you very much.

And she would get in touch with her mother later, after she'd had a little time to decide exactly what she wanted to say to her.

The evening went by—a goodly portion of it spent joyfully in Quinn's strong arms. After he left, she had trouble falling asleep. She couldn't stop stewing over what to tell her mom.

Somehow, in the morning, she slept through her alarm. That left her rushing to get ready and out the door in time to get the showroom opened by nine.

Her mother called the showroom number at ten. "Sweetheart, there you are!"

Chloe still wasn't ready to deal with her. "Mom. Glad you're home safe. Can't talk now. You know that. I'm at work."

"But how am I supposed to get hold of you if you won't answer your—?"

"Mom, I have another call," she outright lied. "I'll call you this evening, I promise."

"But—"

"Gotta go. I'll call. Promise."

Her mother was still protesting as Chloe hung up the phone. She knew time was running out. She was going to have to stop being such a coward. All day long, in the back of her mind, she rehearsed the things she would say when she called back that night.

I've been seeing Quinn Bravo. I care for him, Mom.
Deeply. He's asked me to marry him and I am seriously
considering telling him yes.

It all sounded so simple. It was…what people did.
They found each other and they fell for each other and
realized they didn't want to be apart. So they got married and raised a family.

Why shouldn't she have that—and with the right man
this time? With a good man, a strong man. A man who
cared about more than money and power and *things*. A
man who considered her a whole person, with a heart and
mind of her own, not just his most prized possession who
looked good on his arm and had great taste and could
work a room with the best of them.

Short answer: she absolutely *should* have that. And
she *would* have it. With Quinn.

By the time she locked up the showroom and went
home, she was all fired up to get it over with. To call
her mother and tell her simply and proudly that she and
Quinn were together.

But as it turned out, no call was necessary. When she
pulled into her driveway, her mother's Mercedes SUV
was parked in the side space next to the garage.

Chloe's stomach lurched at the sight, which was so
pitiful it made her want to throw her head back and
scream. But she didn't scream. She drew in a slow breath
and told herself to man up. It was her life and she was
going to live it for herself, not her mother. She would tell
her mom the simple truth about her and Quinn and that
would be that.

But then, as she left the garage by the breezeway door
and caught sight of her mother waiting on the front step,
it became crystal clear from the tight, furious expres-

sion on Linda Winchester's face that she already knew about Quinn.

Chloe's steps faltered. Only for a second, though. She quickly caught herself, straightened her shoulders and kept right on walking. "Mom. I don't remember you mentioning that you would be dropping by."

"Oh, please." Her mother gave her a truly withering glance. "Let me in. I have a few things to say to you and I'm not going to say them on your front step."

Chloe froze with her key raised to unlock the door. "Look, Mother. I don't want to—"

"Open the door. Now, please."

The temptation was so powerful to tell her mother right then and there that this was *her* house and *she* would decide who did or didn't enter it.

But then again, well, Linda Winchester wasn't the only one who had a few things to say. And she wasn't the only one who preferred to have this out in private.

So she unlocked the door. Her mother brushed past her as she disarmed the alarm.

Carefully, quietly, Chloe shut the door. Her mother stood beside the formal dining table, her blond head high, bright spots of color flaming on her cheeks, her lips bloodless with tension.

Chloe almost felt sorry for her. "Look, Mom. Why don't you sit down?"

Linda whipped out the chair at the end of the table and sat in it. She put her hand to her mouth and shut her eyes.

Chloe took the nearest chair. She waited until her mother dropped her hand away from her mouth and opened her eyes again before she said gently, "You're obviously very upset. Please tell me why."

Her mother sucked in a gasp and snapped, "Don't you play coy with me, Chloe."

"I'm not playing coy," Chloe said with a calm that surprised her. "What I'm doing is trying my best not to jump to conclusions."

"All right." With two sharp tugs, Linda straightened the sides of the linen jacket she wore. "Agnes Oldfield dropped by to see me an hour ago. She says it's all over town that you've been seeing Quinn Bravo. She says you went to the Sylvan Inn with him last Friday night, where you told Monique Hightower right to her face that you were…*attracted* to that man ever since high school. Agnes also says that you've been seen having ice cream with him and that child of his. She says that everyone says how…intimate you seem together, that it's obvious something serious is going on between you." Linda pressed her hand flat to her chest, and shook her head fiercely. "I do not believe this. Tell me that none of it is true."

Chloe just stared. God. She'd known this would be bad. But somehow, now that it was actually happening, all she could think was *What are we doing here? How could I have let it get his far? Why didn't I back her down years ago*?

The questions were all too familiar to her. They were the same ones she'd asked herself over and over about her ex-husband.

"Well?" her mother demanded. "What do you have to say for yourself?"

"You know, Mom. I don't think I have to say anything. But I would like to know what happened to *you*? I just don't understand how you got so messed up."

Another indignant gasp. "Excuse me?"

"It's not going to work on me, Mother. Not anymore. All your trumped-up outrage, your sad, small-minded ideas about who's okay and who's not. Your judgments about the right kind of people and the ones who just don't measure up."

"Wait just a minute, now—"

"No. No, I'm not going to wait for you to try and fill my head with more of your small-minded garbage and your snobbish, silly lies."

"Well, I have never—"

"Stop. I mean it. I don't want to hear it, never again. Quinn Bravo is a fine man and I'm not listening to one more word of this ridiculous crap you're dishing out against him. Yes, I am seeing him. And I am *proud* to be seeing him. Also, you should know that I am redoing his house and I'm gratified that he and Manny Aldovino have confidence in my ability to do the job well. In fact, Quinn has asked me to marry him and I am seriously considering saying yes."

"Dear, sweet Lord. Have you lost your mind?"

"No, I have not. I am perfectly sane, saner than I've ever been in my life before. And all that old stuff about Quinn's mother and his father and his father's first wife, all those ancient, ridiculous distinctions between the *real* Bravos and the *bastard* Bravos… Nobody cares about that anymore. Nobody but you—and maybe Monique Hightower and Agnes Oldfield, who both ought to get a life and stay out of mine."

"But you surely can't—"

"Wake up, Mother. Smell the Starbucks. I mean, look at it this way. Haven't you heard? Quinn Bravo's rich now. He's made a big success of his life. You know how much you love a big success."

Linda Winchester paled. "How dare you imply that I care how much money a man makes?"

Chloe knew she had lost it completely when she shouted, "I'm not implying it, I'm saying it straight out!"

Her mother cringed and jerked back in her chair, as though terrified—which Chloe knew very well she was not. "There's no need to shout," Linda said with a wounded sniff. "And I would hardly consider beating other men to a pulp a 'successful' way to make a living. And what about that motherless child of his being raised by that strange old man?"

"Manny is a wonderful person and he's doing a terrific job with Annabelle."

"Oh, please. It doesn't matter how much money he has. Quinn Bravo will never measure up and I raised you to know that."

"Enough." Chloe stood. "What I know, Mother, is that I'm done. I'm finished. I've had enough of your narrow-minded, holier-than-thou, manipulative behavior to last me a lifetime."

Another hot gasp from her mother. "What's happened to you? What's the *matter* with you? You're acting like a crazy person. I brought you up to be better than this."

"Stop. Quit. There's just no point. I want you to leave now. I want you to leave my house and not come back until you've had a serious change in your attitude."

Something happened then. Linda's gaze shifted away. When she looked back at Chloe, she actually seemed worried. Was it possible she'd finally realized she'd gone too far? She said, more softly than before, with a hint of appeasement, "It's only that I don't want you to throw your life away. It's only that you're special. You deserve the best life has to offer. I want that for you. I want *everything* for you."

"I really do want you to go now." Chloe gentled her tone, but didn't waver. "Please."

Linda didn't get up. She only talked faster. "Oh, sweetheart. I know. I understand. You had it all. And you threw it away. But the good news is, if you'll only make a little effort, you and Ted can work through this rough patch and—"

Chloe put up a hand. "Get back with Ted? You can't be serious. I don't believe you, Mother. How many times have I told you I never want to hear his name? How many times have I told you that he hit me and he cheated on me and there is no going back from that? I don't *want* to go back. All I want is never to have to look in his evil, lying face again."

"You're overwrought."

"Oh, you bet I am." She stepped back and pointed at the door. "Please leave my house. Now."

Finally, her mother stood—and kept on talking. "Can't you see? That new wife of his? She's a pale imitation. She can't hold a candle to you. Ted realizes that now. And you know that you're exaggerating about his behavior, making a big drama out of a little marital spat or two."

"Wait." Chloe really, truly could not believe her ears. "What did you say?"

"I said, you're making a big drama of—"

"'He *realizes* that now'? How could you know what Ted Davies realizes?"

"Well, sweetheart, now listen. You really need to settle down, so that we can speak of this reasonably."

"Reasonably?" Chloe echoed in a near whisper. The awful truth had hit her like a boot to the head. Her ears were ringing. "You've been in touch with him, haven't you? You've been *encouraging* him."

Linda got right to work blowing her off. "Well, I… You know I only want what's best for you and I—"

"You've given him my address, haven't you?"

"Oh, don't be foolish. It's not as if you're in hiding."

"So you did give him my address."

Linda just wouldn't give it up and answer the question. She let out a low sound of complete disdain. "Don't make such an issue of it. Anyone could find out where you live with a minimum of effort."

"But Ted didn't have to make *any* effort, right? Because you'll tell him whatever he wants to know." She grabbed her mother's arm. "That does it. You're leaving."

Linda squealed. "What are you doing?" She slapped at Chloe. "Let go of me. You're *hurting* me..." The tears started then.

Chloe ignored them. She pulled her mother to the door, yanked it open and shoved her over the threshold.

Linda sobbed, "How can you do this to me? You're breaking my heart."

Chloe's answer was to firmly shut the door in her face.

Chapter Seven

That night, it took Quinn an extra half hour to chase off all the monsters and get Annabelle settled in bed. He performed his monster-removing duties happily. Partly because he was a total pushover for his little girl. And partly because he knew she needed the extra attention on her first night in her temporary bedroom in the log house across the street from Chloe.

After Annabelle finally went to sleep, he and Manny took beers out to the back deck, where they touched base on the usual household stuff, finances and the move.

They were just wrapping up when his cell chimed. A text. From Chloe. The first, he realized, that he'd ever gotten from her.

That made him smile—initially. And then he had to deal with the words in the little conversation bubble. At least it was only one sentence: Can you come over now?

Unease curled through him. Something in the starkness of the question didn't sit right. Chloe was generally so gracious and well mannered, the kind of woman to offer a drink and ask a man how his day had been before ever getting down to what she needed from him.

Manny asked, "Chloe?"

"Yeah." Texting was not his best event. He debated the option of turning up the sound on his text-to-speech app and voice-texting her back. Or he could just call her. But she was only across the street and he felt an urgency to get to her. He rose.

"Something wrong, Crush?"

Quinn clasped Manny's shoulder. "Probably nothing."

Manny reached up, patted his hand and let him go without a single wiseass remark.

Chloe must have been standing at the door, peering through the peephole, because she whipped it open before Quinn could raise his hand to knock. One look at her too-pale face and shadowed, red-rimmed eyes and Quinn knew his instincts had been right. Something had gone way wrong.

"Quinn." She grabbed for him.

He stepped inside, gathered her close and shoved the door shut with his heel.

"Quinn…" She curled against him, tucking her golden head under his chin, her slim arms clutching tight around him, as though she wanted to crawl right inside skin.

It freaked him out a little to see her so out of control. That only happened when he had her naked in bed. The rest of the time, she was the queen of smooth, hard to ruffle. Something had really spooked her. He stroked her hair and rubbed her back and reassured her with low, soothing words. "I'm here. It's okay now, all right? You just hold on tight…"

She burrowed even closer against him and confessed in a torn whisper, "I never, ever had the guts to stand up to her and now it's come down to this. Oh, I hate myself. I'm such a wuss. It shouldn't have gotten to this, I should have stopped her a long time ago. I—"

"Shh," he soothed. "Shh, now. Take a breath, a long, slow one…"

Obedient as a cowed and frightened child, she took a long, deep one and let it out nice and slow. "Oh, Quinn…" A sob escaped her.

He caught her beautiful face between his hands, tipped it up so he could see her haunted eyes again and took an educated guess. "This is about your mother?"

She hitched in a ragged breath and nodded. "After tonight, she's out of my life. I never want to see her again."

"Whoa," he said gently. "Come on, now, angel. Whatever she did, she *is* your mother."

Chloe pursed up her lips and stuck out her chin. "Don't even remind me."

"I'm only saying, whatever happened with her, give her a little time. She'll come around."

"Oh, you don't know her, Quinn," she insisted. "You don't know her at all." She sounded downright pissed off.

Which wasn't so bad, he decided. He'd take pissed off over brokenhearted and out of control any day of the week. "Hey." He stroked her hair some more, brushed a quick kiss across her sweet, trembling mouth. "You gonna talk to me? *Really* talk to me? Because I need a better idea of what happened before I can do much more than hold you and tell you it'll be okay."

"It was awful. We went at each other. She was like one of those crazed, jealous girlfriends on *The Jerry Springer Show*." Chloe shut her eyes and sucked in another slow, careful breath. "And I wasn't much better."

Now, there was an image. Chloe and Linda Winchester going at it on *The Jerry Springer Show.* "Come on. Make some coffee or something. You can tell me what happened."

A few minutes later, they sat on the sofa. Chloe sipped the hot tea she'd made for herself. "She was waiting on the front step when I got home from work, and she was furious."

It didn't take a genius to figure out why. "Someone told her about you and me."

"That's right. She…" Chloe met his eyes then. "I don't even know how to tell you how awful she was."

"It's okay. You don't have to give me a blow-by-blow. She's never thought much of me or of my family and we knew that from the first."

"I, well, I want you to know that I didn't back down, Quinn. I didn't evade, either. For the first time in my life I stood right up to her. I told her I was seeing you and I intended to *keep* seeing you and that she'd better accept that."

"But she wouldn't accept it."

"No. We yelled at each other. I realized it was going nowhere and I asked her to leave. That was when she let it slip that she's been in touch with my ex-husband." Chloe's gaze slid away. "I hit the ceiling and threw her out." She fell silent, and she still wasn't looking at him.

He waited. When she didn't volunteer any more, he said, "It's probably about now that you should tell me whatever it is you're *not* telling me about your ex-husband."

She did face him then. And she looked stricken. In a small voice, she said, "I don't even know where to begin." He took her mug from her and set it on the low table. Then he hooked an arm around her shoulders and pulled her close to his side. She crumpled against him. "Oh, God…"

He pressed a kiss into her sweet-smelling hair. "It doesn't matter where you start. I'm not going anywhere until you've told me everything I need to know."

She let out a small, sad little sound. "All my life, all I wanted was to be my mother's good little girl. And look where that's gotten me…"

Quinn said nothing. He held her close.

Finally, hesitantly, she told him the story. "I met Ted Davies at Stanford in my sophomore year. He was four years older than me, in law school. And he was everything my mother raised me to want. Handsome and charming, already rich, from a powerful California family, bound for a successful career as a corporate lawyer. I saw him as perfect husband material, and he saw me as exactly the right wife to stand by him as he climbed to the top. We got married in a gorgeous wine country wedding at the end of my senior year and I went to work being his wife, which both of us considered a full-time job. It was all going so well until Ted lost his temper. He'd decided I'd been too friendly to one of the partners at his office Christmas party. We had a fight. We'd been married for a little more than two years. That was the first time he hit me." She tipped her head up and looked at Quinn then.

He knew that look. She was checking to see how he was taking it. He met her eyes and stroked her hair and didn't let her see what was going on inside him. He was a simple man, really, especially when it came to stuff like this. A simple man who wanted to track down that jackass she'd married and beat his face in for him.

Chloe lowered her head again and tucked herself against his chest. "I left him."

"Good."

She glanced up again. He was ready for that. Playing it easy and accepting for all he was worth, he kissed the tip of her elegant nose. With a sigh, she settled again. "Ted…wooed me back. He went into counseling for anger management to prove to me that he was a changed man."

"But he wasn't."

"I'll say this. He didn't hit me again for a long time, though his scary temper was increasingly in evidence as the next four years went by. Three years ago, I found out he was having an affair with a college student, an intern at his firm. I confronted him. When he couldn't convince me that he was totally innocent and that I was only being a small-minded, jealous wife, he lost it. He punched me in the face hard enough to bloody my nose and blacken both eyes. I left him. And after that, I was done. No cajoling or high-powered charm offensive or promises that he'd get more counseling could sway me. I sued for divorce. As it happened, he was still seeing the other woman—and she wanted to be his wife. So I got my divorce and a nice settlement. And Ted got a new, younger wife. And except for how I still feel guilty that I didn't press assault charges against him, that should have been the end of it, right?"

He rubbed a soothing hand up and down her arm. "But it wasn't."

"I tried to keep going in Southern California. But then Ted started coming around again, talking reconciliation, as if I would even let him near me, as if he didn't have a wife waiting at home. I decided I needed to make a new start—or rather, I realized what I really wanted was to come back where I began and try to get it right this time."

He tipped her chin up then and kissed her.

She said shyly, "I do feel like I'm finally getting it right, Quinn. Getting it right with you."

Those fine words dampened his carefully masked fury against the abusive loser she'd married, enough that he kissed her again. And then he asked, "So you're sure that your mother's been in contact with this guy?"

"She wouldn't admit it straight out, but yes. I'm sure she has. She told me how he wants to get back together with me—and my mother's all for that. That was when I finally threw her out. I'm done with her, Quinn. Finished."

Quinn blew out a slow breath. He was no more a fan of Linda Winchester than Linda was of him. And it turned his stomach that the woman would go behind Chloe's back and encourage the man who'd hurt her.

But there had been deep and painful rifts in his own family, especially back in the day when his father refused to choose between Sondra Oldfield Bravo and Quinn's mother. It wasn't all roses now, but it was better. Since returning to Justice Creek, he'd discovered he actually *liked* his half siblings. That couldn't have happened if they'd refused to give each other a chance.

"Still," he said. "There's a bond there, a strong one, between you and your mother."

"It's broken. Broken beyond repair."

"Chloe, she's family. You gotta keep that in mind, you know? I'm not saying just forgive her and act like nothing happened. But try to be open, okay? Give it time and see if she comes around, makes amends."

"I wish I could be as accepting and patient as you are."

Quinn had to stifle a grunt of disbelief when she said that. Yeah, he might be willing to be patient with her mother. But Chloe's ex? He'd like to meet good old Ted in a dark alley some night. Only one of them would come out, and it wouldn't be Davies.

Chloe snuggled in close again. "Can we just…leave the subject of my mother alone for now?"

"Sure. But I got a question."

She must have picked up something not all that accepting in his tone, because she pushed free of his arms and scooted back to the other couch cushion. "What?"

"You heard from this Ted character since you moved back to Justice Creek?"

Chloe cleared her throat. A definite tell. "No. He, um, hasn't called."

Quinn knew then that the guy *had* been in contact with her. He reminded her, "You and me, we got something special. And I know when you're not being straight with me."

She wrapped her arms around herself and pleaded with those pretty blue eyes. "You have to promise me you won't do anything, won't…go after him or anything."

Quinn's pulse leaped. He couldn't keep a promise like that. "You just gotta tell me what he did, Chloe. You know that you do, you know that's how we need to be with each other. We need to tell the truth to each other—and *then* we can decide what to do about it."

She swallowed. Hard. "All right. One time."

"You've heard from him one time?"

"Yes. He sent me flowers. With a short note that said how flowers remind him of me and he was sorry it didn't work out…"

There was more, he was certain. He pushed for it. "And?"

"The note also said that he, um…missed me. I threw everything—the vase, the flowers, that damn note, too—in the trash compactor and ground it all to bits."

"When was that?"

"A week ago. Last Wednesday night."

He wanted to pick up her tea mug from the table and hurl it at the far wall. But he kept it together and said levelly, "That was the night we sat out on your deck and talked for two hours."

She gazed at him warily now. "What are you getting at?"

"I wish you had told me then—or any day or night since then."

"That's not fair and you know it. It's been happening pretty fast with us. Think about it. I just couldn't tell you, didn't even know *how* to tell you—not the night it happened or the next day, or the day after that. I can barely talk about it now."

She had a point. He knew it. And really, he only wanted to neutralize any threat to her. "I don't blame you, angel." He said it softly, without heat. Because it was true. "No way do I blame you."

Her sweet face crumpled. "You mean that?"

"You know I do." He reached for her. She let out a small cry and allowed him to wrap his arms around her again. He held her tight, loving the way she felt, so soft in all the right places. "That's it, then? That's the only move he's made on you since you came back home?"

"Yes. That's it."

"Did you call him and tell him to leave you alone?"

"Uh-uh. You have no idea how many times in the past I told him to leave me alone. That only seemed to encourage him."

"I hear that. So, then, don't engage him." He lifted her hand and pressed his lips to the back of it. "Did you go to the police?"

"And tell them what? That my ex-husband sent me flowers out of the blue and a nice little note?"

"Don't get defensive. I agree that you don't have anything to charge the creep with. I just want to be sure, to know everything that happened, to know exactly where we stand with this piece of crap."

"We?" She pushed away from him again, smoothed the yellow skirt of her pretty summer dress over her knees and then looked him straight in the eye. "Quinn. Ted is in no way your problem. This thing with him is for me to solve. I will not drag you into my mess. I don't want you going after him, or approaching him, or contacting him or getting near him, ever. I need your word on that."

He would give her anything—the world on a gold platter. But not this. "That guy needs to know you're not alone anymore. He needs to know someone's got your back."

"I couldn't care less what *he* needs, Quinn. I'm talking about what *I* need. And that is to know I can tell you my hardest secrets and trust that you won't go racing off to solve all my problems for me in your own way. Because they are *my* problems and I'm the one who gets the final say when it comes to dealing with them. It's about respect, and you know it. You have to respect me and let *me* figure out how to mop up the mess I created. Please."

He really hated that what she said made sense. "You *will* tell me, if he does *anything*, if you hear so much as a word from him again?"

"I will, yes." She folded her hands on her knees. "And you will honor my wishes and let me handle this in my own way?"

He scraped both hands down his face. "You got me up against the ropes here."

"Because you *do* respect me. I know you only want

to protect me and you have no idea how much I love that about you."

Love. It was a big word. And it was also the first time she'd used it in reference to him. Quinn liked the way it sounded coming out of that fine mouth of hers. He liked it a lot.

What he didn't like was not being allowed to teach Ted Davies an important life lesson. Then again, guys like that always managed to get what was coming to them eventually. Quinn fervently hoped he'd have the honor of taking Ted to church when the time came.

"Quinn?" she asked, all breathless and hopeful. "I need your word that you'll leave Ted alone."

Damn it to hell. He gave it up. "All right. For now, for as long as he never tries to get in touch with you again, you got my word."

Chloe was no fool.

She fully understood what it cost Quinn to make her that promise. He'd done a really good job of hiding his anger at Ted. But already, in the short time they'd been together, she'd learned to read him. He wanted to go after Ted, he *needed* to do that, needed to step forward and be her protector.

What woman wouldn't appreciate that in a man?

But he'd done protectiveness one better. He'd agreed to go against what he needed to do and leave Ted alone. Because she'd asked him to. And if she hadn't already been halfway in love with him, well, that he *had* made that promise kind of sealed the deal as far as she was concerned.

"Thank you," she whispered, taking his big hand, turning it over and smoothing his beefy fingers open.

"Thank you…" She bent close and pressed a kiss in the center of his rough, hot palm.

"Let's just hope we've seen the last of him," Quinn muttered gruffly.

She couldn't agree more. And not only because she wanted nothing to do with her ex. Now there was Quinn to worry about. If Ted made another move on her, convincing Quinn to stay out of it was going to be exponentially tougher.

But they'd spent altogether too much of their evening on unhappy subjects. She forced a brighter tone. "First my mother, then Ted. Let's forget about both of them for now, huh?" She reached up and smoothed the thick brown hair off his forehead. "Now I want it to be just you and me, here on the sofa, doing whatever comes naturally."

He studied her face for a moment, his head tipped to the side. And then he kicked off his shoes. She followed suit, sliding off her sandals and pushing them under the coffee table.

"Come here." He took her by the shoulders, turned her and settled her with her head in his lap.

Chloe stared up at him, feeling better already. The hard things had been said. And now it was just her and Quinn, alone for the evening. He traced the curves of her eyebrows with a slow finger and then caught a lock of her hair and wrapped it around his hand the way he liked to do.

She said, "I hope I didn't drag you away from anything important at home…"

He shook his head. "Annabelle's all tucked in bed. Manny and I were just having a beer on the deck."

"Do you still want to marry me?" The words kind of popped out. She'd hardly known she would say them— until she did.

He gave her his bad-boy half smile. "Oh, yeah. But I'm not pushing. You decide what you want and you do it in your own time."

"Even after all the grim stuff I told you tonight? I'm not sure I'm such a good bet, Quinn."

He unwrapped her hair from around his fingers—and then twined it right back again. "You're not your mother and it's not your fault that your ex is a psycho dog. You *are* a good bet, angel. You're a fine woman with a big heart, the best there is."

His generous words warmed her, made a glow down inside her that all the trials of the afternoon and evening couldn't dim.

I think I'm falling in love with you, Quinn.

It sounded so right inside her head. But she wasn't quite ready to say it out loud yet. Talk of love still had some taint for her. It still held ugly echoes of the past.

She shut her eyes and drifted, cradled, safe, with her head in Quinn's lap.

Marriage. To Quinn.

Was she ready for that? They'd been together such a short time and she'd messed up so badly before. How could she be certain?

She opened her eyes.

And he was gazing down at her, steady. Sure. Not having to say anything, just being there with her.

When she looked in his eyes, her doubts about herself and her future and her iffy judgment just melted away. When she looked in Quinn's eyes, she *was* sure.

And come on. She'd dated Ted for a year before she said yes to him. And then it was another year until their lavish wedding. She'd given herself plenty of time to really *know* Ted. She'd done everything right.

And still, it all went wrong. Ted was the man her mother wanted for her.

And Quinn?

It was so simple. Quinn was the one *she* wanted for herself. He was *her* choice, her second chance to get it right. She trusted him. She knew he would be good to her, that she would be good for him—and for Annabelle and Manny, too.

Together, they could make a full, rich life, the life she'd always wanted. The life she'd given up hope that she would ever find.

Until now. Until Quinn.

He unwound her hair again. And she sat up and took his arm and wrapped it across her shoulders. He gathered her closer. She drew her legs up onto the sofa and folded them to the side so she was facing him. Looking right into those wonderful eyes, she said, "Well, I've decided, then. And my decision is…" She stretched up enough to nip his scruffy jaw with her teeth. "Yes."

For once, he actually looked taken completely off guard. "What did you say?"

"I said yes, Quinn. I will marry you. I want it to be a small, simple wedding, just family and close friends. And I want it to be soon."

"Chloe." He took her face between those big hands. "Seriously? You're sure?" He looked so vulnerable right then, as if he couldn't quite believe she really meant it.

She did mean it. "Yes, I am very sure."

"Damn," he whispered prayerfully.

He kissed her, a kiss that curled her bare toes and created that incomparable heavy, hot yearning down in the core of her. And then he scooped her up in those big arms of his and carried her to her bedroom.

Late into the night, he showed her exactly how happy her decision had made him.

Dawn was breaking when he left her. She stood out on her front porch in a robe and slippers, watching him walk across the street to his temporary home, knowing her hair needed combing and her eyes were low and lazy. She was fully aware that she had the look of a woman thoroughly and repeatedly satisfied—and she didn't care in the least who saw her.

She'd made her decision. She was marrying Quinn and finally getting the life she'd always dreamed of.

Chapter Eight

At the showroom a few hours later, Chloe called Tai and asked her to come in early.

At ten, Quinn picked her up. They drove to Denver, where they had lunch and he bought her a beautiful engagement ring and a platinum wedding ring to match. She bought him a ring, too, a thick platinum band that she couldn't wait to slip on his finger when the big day came. She was back at her showroom by four.

That evening, just as she was letting herself in the front door, the house phone rang. She saw it was her parents' number and let it go to the machine.

A few minutes later, she checked to see what her mother had said. But it turned out it was her dad. He'd left a two-sentence message: "Chloe, this is your dad. Please call me."

She did, right then.

He asked her if she was all right and Chloe told him that she would be fine.

Doug Winchester said, "Your mother's just broken-hearted over what happened last night."

Chloe refused to let him play the guilt card on her. "We don't see eye-to-eye, Mom and me. And I don't think that either of us will be changing our positions anytime soon."

"She loves you. You know that. *I* love you."

"Thanks, Daddy. I love you, too. But sometimes love really can't make everything right. Not with Mom, anyway. With Mom, it's her way or nothing. And I'm through doing things her way. In fact, Quinn's asked me to marry him and I've said yes."

The line went dead silent. Then her father asked cautiously, "Isn't this a little sudden?"

She resisted the urge to say something snappish. "I care for him deeply, Dad. It's what I want."

"You're sure?"

"I am."

Another silence. And then her father had the good grace to say that he hoped she would be happy. "I think I'll wait a few days to tell your mother about your engagement, though."

"Right now, Dad, I don't care if you tell her or not."

"Chloe. You don't mean that."

She didn't argue. What was the point? "I'll call and let you know about the wedding. It's going to be small and simple." Nothing like the three-ring circus in Sonoma when she'd married Ted. "I hope you can come. Quinn wants me to be patient with Mom, so I'm going to give it a little time before I decide whether I'm willing to have her at the wedding."

Another deep silence from her dad. Then, "Let's just see how things go, shall we?"

Chloe agreed that would be wise. They said goodbye.

A few hours later, when Quinn came over, she cried

a little for her fractured family. He held her and told her
it would all turn out all right. Somehow, when he said it,
she almost believed it.

Friday morning first thing, Nell Bravo dropped by
Chloe's showroom. Chloe broke the big news and showed
off her gorgeous ring.

Nell said, "So, then. This makes it official. You're gonna
be my sister. And that means we'll have to bury the hatchet
permanently, you and me."

"You know, you really scare me when you talk about
hatchets."

Nell laughed and grabbed Chloe in a hug and waltzed
her in and out of the various carpet and flooring displays.
Then Quinn's sister confessed, "I already knew. Quinn
told me this morning. And I'm here to find out when
you're breaking for lunch so I can get a table at the Sylvan Inn for you and me and my sisters."

Chloe met the Bravo sisters at the Sylvan Inn at one.
There were four of them. Clara and Elise were the daugh-
ters of Franklin Bravo's first wife, Sondra. Jody's and
Nell's mother was the notorious Willow Mooney Bravo,
who'd been Frank's mistress during most of his marriage
to Sondra. The day after Sondra Bravo's funeral, Willow married Frank. He moved her right into the mansion
he'd built for Sondra. Frank Bravo's refusal to observe
even a minimal period of mourning after Sondra's passing caused no end of shock and outrage in the angry
hearts of the judgmental types in town, Chloe's mother
first among them.

Tracy Winham, Elise's best friend and business partner, joined them, too. And so did Rory Bravo-Calabretti,
a cousin to the Bravo sisters. Rory was an actual princess
from a tiny country called Montedoro. But Rory didn't

act like a princess. She loved Justice Creek and she was down-to-earth and lots of fun. Recently she'd decided to make her home in America. She lived with her fiancé, Walker McKellan, at Walker's guest ranch not far from town.

As a matter of fact, all the Bravo women were lots of fun. Even more so after a couple of glasses of the champagne Nell had ordered to toast Chloe and Quinn and their future happiness together. Chloe never drank alcohol at lunch. After all, she still had half a day of work ahead and she preferred to be alert and clearheaded on the job.

But today, she drank the champagne—more than she should have. And she had a fabulous time sharing stories about the old days with Quinn's sisters.

"Quinn was always so moody," said Jody, and everyone nodded. "He was mad at everything and just about everybody."

"But even then there was a certain sweetness about him," said Clara, who was Sondra's oldest daughter and considered the family peacemaker.

Back in the day, when the two sides of Frank's family were constantly at odds, Clara was the one who kept trying to get them to make peace and come together. She and Quinn and Chloe were the same age.

"I remember," Clara said, "when we were in Miss Oakleaf's class, first grade. Remember, Chloe?"

"Yes, I do. Miss Oakleaf was so pretty. I wanted to be just like her when I grew up."

"Oh, me, too," Clara agreed.

"She pinned her hair up in a twist and she always looked so elegant. And she wore high heels and pencil skirts." Chloe frowned. "Were they even called pencil skirts back then?"

Clara considered. "Straight skirts, I think. And yeah. Miss Oakleaf was a beauty. Quinn had a big crush on her."

"She was patient with him," Chloe said softly, remembering how he struggled to keep up with the rest of the class.

Clara remembered, too. "He would get mad and act up and she would talk to him so gently."

"And then," said Chloe, "the Hershey's Kisses started appearing on her desk every morning..."

Clara took up the story. "Just a few of them, lined up in their shiny silver foil wrappers, waiting there for Miss Oakleaf on her desk pad at the beginning of every day."

"No one knew who was leaving them," said Chloe.

And Clara said, "Until Freddy Harmon spotted Quinn in the act. Freddy spied on Quinn through the window, didn't he, and saw him sneak in and put three Kisses on Miss Oakleaf's desk?"

"That's right," Chloe replied softly. "Quinn was so humiliated..." She shook her head, aching for the troubled little boy he'd once been.

Jody said, "The way I heard it, he went ballistic."

Clara nodded. "He chased Freddy around the playground till he caught him, and then he beat the crap out of him. For that, Quinn was suspended for two weeks. Looking back on our elementary school years, it seems like he spent more time suspended or in detention than he ever spent in class."

They all laughed. They could afford to laugh about it now that Quinn was a grown man who'd built himself a fine, productive life.

Nell asked, "Remember that time he and Jamie and Dare got into it on the playground?" James and Darius were Clara's and Elise's full brothers, Sondra's sons.

Elise nodded. "It was two against one. Plus, Jamie and Dare were older and bigger. But Quinn just wouldn't give up and go down."

Rory shook her head. "It's so strange, knowing him now, to hear what a troublemaker he used to be."

"By the time he was twelve or so," Clara said, "no one would fight with him. By then, they all knew that he would never quit. If you took on Quinn Bravo, it was going to be long and ugly and there would be way too much blood."

"But look how he turned out," Tracy piped up. "Rich and successful, with a beautiful daughter, about to marry the one and only Chloe Winchester." Tracy raised her glass and everyone followed suit. "To Chloe. You go, girl."

Chloe blushed a little. "Aww."

Nell shook her gorgeous head of auburn hair. "Chloe. Seriously. You and Quinn? Never woulda seen that coming."

Chloe beamed at her future sister-in-law, her heart full of fondness, her brain pleasantly hazy with the champagne and the good family feelings. She really was starting to feel seriously bondy with Nell. Was it only five days ago that they'd squared off in the trailer at Bravo Construction?

"Heads up, my sisters," Elise whispered out of the side of her mouth. "Don't look now, but here comes trouble."

Trouble in the tall, thin form of Monique Hightower. Wearing jeans, a silk top and giant sunglasses, Monique had just breezed in the door. She said something to the hostess and then spotted the Bravo women at the round table in the center of the dining room. Slowly, she eased the big sunglasses up to rest on her head. And then she smiled.

And then she came striding on over. "Hey, Clara, Elise, everyone. Looks like a party…"

Nell said, "It is. We are celebrating."

About then, Monique zeroed in on Chloe. "Chloe. Well. How's every little thing?"

Chloe raised her champagne glass—with her left hand, so that her engagement diamond caught the light and sparkled. "Remember how I told you if I played my cards right, I might have a chance with Quinn?"

Somebody snickered. Chloe thought it was Elise, but it could have been Tracy.

Monique's eyes got wider. "Wow. That's, uh…" For once, she actually seemed at a loss for words. Chloe savored the moment.

Then Nell instructed, "Pull yourself together, Monique. Quinn and Chloe are getting married. You need to wish my future sister-in-law a life of love and happiness."

Monique sent Nell a quelling glance that had zero effect on Quinn's baby sister. Nell just rolled her eyes and drank more champagne as Monique trotted out another big, fake smile and a too-perky "Best wishes, Chloe. Quinn's a lucky man."

"Thank you, Monique."

Clara, ever the peacemaker, offered, "Monique, why don't you join us for a glass of champagne?"

Everyone went dead quiet then. They'd been having such a great time and Monique would have them trying to remember to watch what they said, because anything Monique heard was fair game for her gossip mill.

Then Monique sighed. "Wish I could. But I got called in early. I need to change and get to work."

"That's too bad." Somehow Nell kept a straight face when she said it.

By then, Monique had recovered her equilibrium.

"Chloe. That ring is spectacular. And truly, I'm so happy for you."

"Monique. What can I say? Thank you again. That's so nice to hear." And strangely enough, it kind of was. Chloe had the definite warm fuzzies at the moment. She was crazy about the Bravo women, crazy about Quinn. Crazy about *everyone*. She was even crazy about Monique, who couldn't keep a confidence if her life depended on it.

Champagne at lunchtime? She should try it more often.

Nobody said a word until Monique disappeared into the kitchen. And then Nell tapped her water glass with her spoon. "So. Engagement party. We need to throw one."

Chloe started to protest that they didn't have to.

But then again, that could be fun, right?

How much fun had she had in her life, really?

Not enough. She'd always been mama's good girl, a busy little bee, working so hard to do everything right, to get straight As and get into a great college and find the perfect husband to make a perfect life.

There'd been no time for fun, not when she was so laser-focused on chasing the life her mother wanted for her.

And after her marriage to Ted? Well, it only went downhill from there. Hard to have fun when your life that looked so perfect on the outside was empty at the core, when you lived with a man you couldn't trust not to hurt you.

But now she had Quinn and anything seemed possible. All the good things: passion and tenderness and lots of laughter. And sisters to call her own.

And, for the first time, champagne at lunch.

Chloe let Quinn's sisters plan the party. She smiled and nodded and giggled a lot.

Nell leaned close to her. "Better cut back on the bubbly, baby."

And Chloe giggled some more. But she took Nell's advice and started drinking ice water. By three-thirty, when they left the restaurant, she was almost sober.

They filed out to the parking lot. There were hugs and cheek kisses. Chloe thanked them all profusely.

Nell tapped her shoulder. "You still look a little high. Ride with me. You can get your car later."

So just to be on the safe side, she let Nell take her back to the showroom. When Nell pulled in at the curb, Chloe leaned across the seats and hugged her good and hard. "I'm so glad you're going to be my sister. I never had a sister before."

Nell hugged her back. "Well, now you've got four— five, including Tracy, who always gets insulted if we don't include her."

That evening, Manny went to Boulder to visit his girlfriend. Quinn and Annabelle picked Chloe up at the showroom and took her back to the restaurant to get her car.

Then she joined them at the log house. They had pizza. And after Annabelle was all ready for bed, they watched *Frozen*, which Annabelle seemed to know by heart.

She kept popping in with "Look out!" or "Watch this!" just before something surprising would happen.

Quinn finally had to pause the movie and remind her that it was no fun to watch a movie when little girls were shouting.

Annabelle was sweetly contrite. She turned to Chloe.

"I'm sorry, Chloe. I'm not s'posed to do that. But I get so 'cited!"

Chloe said, "Well, maybe if you don't do it again, your dad will let us watch the rest."

Annabelle turned those big brown eyes on Quinn. "Daddy, I promise I will be quiet."

She managed to get through the rest of the movie without a single exclamation. And by the end, she had edged up close to Chloe on the sofa and rested her head against Chloe's arm. Chloe treasured that small, perfect moment: the first time Annabelle had leaned on her.

It took a while to get the little girl to bed for the night. Quinn spent twenty minutes or so tucking her in. Then, half an hour later, she came out carrying a ratty blanket and an ancient-looking one-eyed teddy bear and demanded that he chase the monsters away. Quinn scooped her up in his arms, blanket, bear and all. He sent Chloe a sheepish look before heading upstairs to Annabelle's bedroom.

"I think she'll stay in bed now," he said when he returned a few minutes later. He confessed that he enjoyed chasing monsters. "It's more of a game with us than anything."

"Don't even think you need to explain," Chloe reassured him. "It looked like you were both having fun and she didn't seem scared in the least."

"Manny says I'm a sucker for Annabelle's monster act."

Chloe chuckled. "Sometimes being a sucker is a good thing."

"I'm going to tell Manny you said that."

They sat on the sofa in the living room in front of the unlit fireplace, with the lights on low. He reached over and ran a finger along the curve of her cheek.

She shivered a little in pleasure, remembering that first night, when he'd come up the hill to her. His daughter had been on his mind that night. "Did she ever have more questions for you about her mom?"

He idly smoothed a curl of her hair back over her shoulder. "Not yet. Just about every night, I think she's going to bring it up. But then she doesn't."

"Give her time."

"I just hope when she does that I don't blow it."

"No way can you blow it, Quinn. You love her and she loves you. She feels safe and protected. And you give her space, you really do. She's allowed to be a little girl, to let her imagination run a little wild…" Chloe felt kind of wistful suddenly.

And Quinn picked up on that. "Hey…" He touched her mouth, traced the bow of her upper lip. "Why the sad face?"

"I don't know. I had a great time with your sisters today at lunch. And it kind of got me thinking that I never had much fun growing up."

"Too busy trying to please your mom?"

"That's right." She made the edges of her mouth turn up. "But I think I'll look on the bright side. Your sisters will be my sisters. Did I tell you they're throwing us an engagement party? Probably at McKellan's, in the party room upstairs." The popular pub was owned by Ryan McKellan, lifetime best friend of Clara Bravo. Ryan's brother, Walker, was engaged to the family princess, Rory.

"And when is this big event?"

"Tentatively, Saturday night two weeks from tomorrow. Clara said she'd get with Ryan and call me this weekend to firm up the date, location and time."

He hooked an arm around her and drew her close

against his side. His warm lips brushed her hair. "Did you know that Clara and Dalton are getting married in three weeks?"

"I did, yes." Clara had a baby daughter, Kiera Anne, with Dalton Ames, president of Ames Bank and Trust. From what Chloe had heard, Clara had taken her time saying yes to her baby's father. But anyone who saw them together could see how much in love they were.

Quinn added, "It'll be a small wedding, Clara said. Food and drinks at her house afterward."

"I heard. Nell said she thought Clara had too much on her plate. So, as soon as Clara sets up our engagement party with Ryan, Nell's taking over to pull the party together."

"You should know we're going to Clara's wedding." He gave her shoulder a squeeze. "You, me, Manny and Annabelle."

"I would love to." She snuggled in, rubbing her cheek against the soft knit fabric of his shirt.

He traced the line of her jaw with his thumb, and then tipped up her chin so she looked in his eyes. "Hey."

"What?"

"The other night, when you said yes?"

"Um?" Oh, those beautiful eyes of his. She could just fall down inside them and never come out.

"You said you wanted it small—and soon. So…" He lowered his wonderful bad-boy lips and brushed a hint of a kiss across her upturned mouth. "What do you say we set the date?"

Set the date. Her heart contracted. Worse, she was suddenly thinking of her mother, and of Ted. Problems. Unresolved problems. *Her* problems that she'd yet to deal with effectively…

But then again, how resolved were things ever going to

get with those two? She might never speak to her mother again. And Ted? The best that could happen with him would be nothing. Ever. For the rest of her life.

So it wasn't about resolving anything; it wasn't about closure...

"Chloe?" Quinn looked at her so tenderly, reminding her suddenly of the little boy who never fit in at school and used to sneak inside before class to leave chocolate candy Kisses for the teacher who'd been kind to him. "So when you said soon, you didn't mean *that* soon?" He asked the question gently.

She let out the breath she hadn't realized she'd been holding. "I'm thinking if we could at least wait until after the engagement party to start planning the wedding?"

His chuckled, the sound low and lovely. "I just don't get it. Why are you dragging your feet? We've been engaged for two whole days now."

She echoed his teasing tone. "People will start thinking we have trouble making commitments."

But then his expression turned serious. "Is it all going too fast for you?"

"I didn't say that." She hated the edge of defensiveness in her tone.

"Hey. I mean it. We can have a long engagement if you want it that way. It's okay with me."

"But I don't *want* a long engagement." It came out as a whine. Dear God, what was the matter with her? Her emotions were bouncing all over the place. She made it worse by grumbling, "And I meant it about a small, simple wedding, too. I really did."

"Easy." He bent close, nipped a kiss against her throat.

"Sorry," she murmured, honestly contrite, not really understanding herself at that moment.

He nuzzled her cheek. "We got no problem here."

Oh, yes, we do. I'm the problem. My mother's a hope-less bitch and I married a psychopath-in-training.

Why would a great guy like Quinn, with everything going for him now, with a good life he'd worked so hard to earn, want to marry someone with her history and track record, anyway?

People always used to treat her like some kind of prize. She was no prize. Not anymore, anyway. In her case, the bloom was seriously off the rose. Perfect Chloe Win-chester? What a joke.

And wait a minute.

Really, she needed to snap out of it.

Where had all these grim thoughts come from?

It was dangerous to start running herself down. Half the battle for sanity and a good life was in keeping her spirits up, fostering a positive attitude.

She'd worked hard to face the tough challenges life had thrown in her path. She'd survived the disaster of her own choice, her own making: her marriage to Ted. She'd fought and fought hard to get free, to make a new life. To hold her head up and move on.

And she'd honestly begun to believe that she'd done it, that she'd put the past behind her.

Until Ted sent her flowers and made her fear deep in her soul that she hadn't seen the last of him, after all. Until her mother showed up on her doorstep spouting such ugliness and rage, revealing such an unforgiveable betrayal, that she'd had no choice but to sever ties with her.

Maybe it wasn't the wedding she was putting off. Maybe she'd had no right to tell Quinn that she'd marry him in the first place.

Maybe she needed to face the fact that he deserved better than her.

"Chloe?"

"Um?"

"We got no problem at all," he said again, more softly, but more firmly, too.

She met his eyes. They were so steady. So knowing and wise. She asked in a tiny, weak, disgusting little voice, "We don't?"

"Uh-uh. We got each other, Chloe. We got it all."

And somehow, when he looked at her like that, when he spoke with such affection and total confidence, she believed him.

She absolutely believed him.

I love you, Quinn. She thought the words and knew that they were true.

If only she felt she had the right to say them out loud.

Chapter Nine

Clara called Saturday afternoon. The engagement party was on for two weeks from that day. Nell called an hour later to go over the guest list.

Monday, the demo began at Quinn's house.

Chloe let Tai run things at the showroom. She put on old jeans and one of Quinn's Prime Sports and Fitness T-shirts and helped Nell and her crew of burly guys bust out some walls. The one between the kitchen and dining area had to go down. And the one between a bonus room and Manny's room needed knocking out, to give him a larger private area. Same thing with the master suite. They were combining it with the smaller bedroom next door. With all the extra space, they would enlarge the master bath and walk-in closet, too.

The men went upstairs. Nell and Chloe took the kitchen. Chloe got right to work attacking that wall. After just one blow, Nell teased her that she was dangerous with a sledgehammer.

Chloe raised the hammer again and sent it crashing through the Sheetrock, making a nice, big raggedy hole that showed light on the other side. "There's something about a demo that makes the whole world seem brighter."

"Whack it down, baby!" Nell made her own big hole.

Upstairs, they heard other hammers demolishing other walls.

"Music to my ears," said Chloe, and gave that wall another serious blow. It was very therapeutic, she decided, to get to beat a wall down.

Since Friday, when she'd realized she wasn't ready to set a wedding date and didn't feel worthy to tell Quinn she loved him, she'd been feeling a little down.

But wielding the hammer helped, made her feel useful and powerful, as though she was getting stuff done. Just what the doctor ordered, without a doubt.

That evening she attended her first Self-Defense for Women class. She got some great tips on how to spot predators and avoid situations where she might be attacked. She almost raised her hand and asked what you did when someone you trusted hauled off and hit you.

But really, she didn't need to ask.

She already knew the answer: you left and you never went back. You started again and rebuilt your life.

And she *was* rebuilding, she reminded herself. Rebuilding in her hometown with a great guy and his sweet little girl. With more family than she'd ever had before, including cool, smart old Manny and a bunch of new sisters, Nell best of all.

A week later, she presented her fairy princess ideas to Annabelle, whose eyes lit up so bright you would have thought Chloe had offered her the moon. "Chloe! I need to hug you." And she reached out and threw her arms around Chloe's legs.

Laughing, Chloe grabbed her up. Annabelle wrapped her legs around Chloe's waist and Chloe spun in a circle, both of them giggling.

When Chloe finally let her go, Annabelle chose the design in lilac, hot pink and purple. The next day, Chloe visited her favorite fabric store and came out with plenty of satin, velvet, bridal tulle, organza, organdy and purple brocade. After the fabric store, she stopped in at the craft store, where she bought special paint and twelve-gauge wire to frame the wings. After lunch, in the studio behind her showroom, she started to work on the costume, taking a break before Tai went home to drive over to Quinn's house down the hill from hers, where the electrician was busy rerouting some of the wiring and Nell's crew was almost finished ripping out the old floors.

She went home that evening feeling good about the remodeling, about Annabelle's fairy princess dress, about pretty much everything. With so much to do and her soon-to-be new family around her, the dark mood brought on by Ted's unwanted flowers and her mother's betrayal had faded. Life seemed bright and full of promise once again.

That Saturday was the engagement party at McKellan's. Quinn hired a babysitter for Annabelle so that Manny could come with them to celebrate. Manny brought his girlfriend, Doris Remy, who was in her midseventies, a widow with fifteen grandchildren and five great-grandsons. Doris had an infectious laugh and loved to dance. She'd once been a Rockette at Radio City Music Hall and she remained slim and spry. McKellan's upstairs party room had a small dance floor, and the Bravos had hired a DJ. Manny and Doris spent most of the evening out on that little square of floor.

Quinn and Chloe danced, too. Chloe also danced with his brothers and with charming Ryan McKellan, who told her she looked happier than he'd ever seen her before. Ryan, like Clara and Quinn, had been in the same grade as Chloe back in school.

Ryan, whom they all called Rye, said, "You always seemed so serious and distant back then."

And she agreed. "Because I was. I had places to go and things to do. Enjoying myself was never on the agenda."

"All that's changed now, though, huh?" Rye asked.

They danced past Quinn, who stood at the upstairs bar with his brother Carter and Clara's fiancé, Dalton Ames. Quinn glanced over as they passed, almost as though he could feel her eyes on him. They shared a smile and a nod and a lovely, sparkly feeling shimmered through her.

And Rye said, "No need to answer. You look at Quinn and your face says it all."

Because I love him, she thought. But she didn't say it. That wouldn't be right, to tell Rye McKellan that she loved Quinn when she'd yet to tell the man himself.

At a little after midnight, with the party in full swing, Quinn's mother, Willow Mooney Bravo, arrived. Chloe, Quinn, Nell and some guy named Ned were sitting at a table not far from the stairs when Willow appeared, looking more beautiful than ever in a white silk blouse with a prim little collar and a black satin skirt, her short blond hair softly curling around her luminous face.

She came straight for their table.

Nell rose. "Mom." Nell and her mother exchanged air kisses. "Big surprise. I thought you were in Miami."

Since her husband's death, Willow traveled a lot. "And miss the party? Never."

Quinn got up and hugged her. She smiled at him so fondly, laying her hand against his cheek, staring up into his eyes. "Congratulations, honey."

"Thanks, Mom."

Chloe rose.

Before she could say a word, Quinn's mom said, "Chloe. So good to see you. You must call me Willow." She took Chloe's hand and laced their fingers together, as though the two of them were BFFs. "Tell you what. Let's steal a few minutes alone and catch up a little."

Catch up? How could she catch up with someone she hardly knew? In her lifetime prior to that moment, she'd exchanged maybe three or four words total with Quinn's mom.

"Mom," Quinn said cautiously. "Are you up to something?"

Willow let out a bright trill of laughter. "What in the world could I be up to?"

Nell made a snorting sound. "Anything's possible. Be nice."

"Of course. I'm *always* nice."

Even Chloe was reasonably certain that was a lie, but she wanted to get off to a good start with Willow. "I'd love to, er, catch up."

"Great." Willow gestured at a hallway across the room. "There's a balcony in back. Let's try that."

Willow led her through the crowd, pausing only for the occasional wave of greeting in the direction of someone she knew.

Accessed through double glass doors, the balcony spanned the back of McKellan's. It had a view of the pub's full parking lot below and the dark humps of the Front Range in the distance.

Willow pulled Chloe to an empty corner. Only then did she release Chloe's hand. She didn't waste time getting right to the point. "So, how are things with your mother?"

Chloe went for honesty. It seemed the only course. "My mother and I aren't speaking. That may be permanent."

Willow gave an elegant shrug. She'd been born in a double-wide southeast of town, but somehow everything she did was elegant. "I can't say I'm sorry. Your mother doesn't speak to me, either, never has. And I like it that way." Chloe had no idea what to say to that, so she said nothing. Willow asked, "Are you saying you and your mother aren't speaking because you're with Quinn?"

"That's part of it, yes. But there are other problems, bigger issues." Chloe shook her head. "And really, that's all I'm going to say about my mother."

Willow rested her slim hands on the railing and stared off toward the mountains. "Quinn has…a tender soul."

"Yes. It's one of the many things I love about him— and Nell's already warned me not to hurt him, so you don't have to go there."

"I didn't think he would ever get married." Willow glanced at Chloe then. "And never to someone like you."

Chloe felt annoyance rising and pointedly did not ask, *What do you mean, someone like me?* Instead, she offered pleasantly, "I think we'll be happy together. We're already happy."

Willow looked toward the mountains again and remarked in a weary tone, "You are a cool one."

"I…" Really, what was she supposed to say to this woman? "What, exactly, do you want from me, Willow?"

Quinn's mother continued her extended study of the distant peaks. "You know, I'm not sure. Except that you never struck me as a person who knew her own mind."

Ouch. That hit a little too close to home. How bad was this conversation going to get? As Chloe asked herself that question, Willow made it worse. "And you were born and raised to marry up, now, weren't you? I just wonder, is Quinn 'up' enough for you? Do you think you're better than he is?"

"Absolutely not." Chloe's voice was hard and final, just as she'd intended it to be.

"You say that as though you mean it."

"I do mean it."

"Wonderful. Then all I need to be sure of is that you can stand up to Linda. You need to be honest with yourself about that. Because if you can't, there will be trouble ahead. Quinn's had enough trouble, enough struggle in his life."

Before Chloe could decide how best to respond to that, Quinn spoke from behind her. "She's doing fine bracing Linda, Mom—not that it's any of your business in the first place."

Quinn to the rescue. Chloe could have hugged him. She turned and slipped her arm through his, finding great comfort in the hard strength of his forearm under her hand, in the solid warmth of him so close to her side.

He slanted her a look both rueful and tender. "How you doing?"

"Just fine. Now."

Willow sighed. "Quinn, you need to stop sneaking up on people."

"I'm in plain sight. You're the one who was looking the other way."

"And it *is* my business," Willow insisted. "You're marrying Linda Winchester's daughter, and Linda and I do not get along. I'm sorry about that, but it's a fact. Chloe needs to be aware of the problem."

"I'm aware," Chloe said. "Painfully so. And I've made it crystal clear to my mother that I run my own life and make my own decisions."

Quinn asked Willow, "Happy now?"

"I only want *you* to be happy."

He put his big hand over Chloe's, a touch of reassurance and support. Really, how did she get so lucky to finally find a man like him? "And I am happy, Mom. Very happy—now, come on. Let's go back inside. It's our party and we want to enjoy it." He offered his mother his other arm.

Willow took it and went in with them. Quinn got her a glass of white wine and she made the rounds, hugging her children, saying hello to various acquaintances. Within half an hour, she was leaving.

"Back to Miami, no doubt," said Nell as Willow slipped away down the stairs. "Or maybe Paris. Or New York. Since Dad died, she never stays here at home for long. I think she's lonely in that big house all by herself."

"She does seem lonely," Chloe agreed. Some of the things Willow had said to her still stung. But the woman *was* alone, and not in a good way. "She seems sad, too."

"Dad was her life. For decades, she battled Sondra to get him for her own. She was always kicking him out in big, dramatic scenes, telling him not to come back until he planned to stay. He would go home to Sondra. But he'd always come around again. And Mom would always take him back, even though he was still wearing his wedding band. Finally, when Sondra died, Mom got what she wanted most of all. For a while, Dad was hers and hers alone. And then he died, too. Now that he's gone, she hardly knows what to do with herself."

"She should sell that house," said Quinn. "It's too big and it's full of stuff that belonged to Sondra."

Nell made a scoffing sound. "Which is why she'll never sell it. In the end, she won out over Sondra. She got Sondra's house and a whole bunch of Sondra's treasures—including her husband." Nell hooked an arm around Chloe and dipped her bright head to rest on Chloe's shoulder. It was a sisterly gesture that warmed Chloe's heart. Nell whispered, "I hope she didn't give you too much crap."

Chloe whispered back, "Look who's talking about giving me crap."

Nell laughed and let her go.

Quinn grumbled, "What are you two whispering about?"

Chloe leaned the other way and kissed him. "Nothing that concerns you."

The following Saturday was Clara and Dalton's wedding.

Quinn sat in the second-row pew with Chloe on one side and Annabelle on the other as Clara and Dalton exchanged their vows. Whenever Quinn glanced at Chloe, she gave him one of those glowing smiles of hers. Annabelle, in a little pink dress with a wide satin bow at the waist and a bell-like skirt, sat up straight with her plump hands folded in her lap, a perfect little lady. Chloe had taken her to Boulder to choose the dress and then made her the cute beaded headband with the big pink silk flower for her hair.

Life was good, Quinn thought. He and Chloe were together every chance they got. Every night last week, they'd shared dinner, the four of them, like the family they were becoming. Chloe did a lot of the cooking, which made everyone happy. Manny had a boatload of great qualities, including a love of cooking. Too bad his cooking sucked.

Yeah. Life was good. Didn't get any better. Though he did feel a twinge of envy as Dalton Ames, his eyes only for Clara, announced proudly, *I do*.

Quinn wanted that, what Dalton and Clara had. He'd never thought it would happen for him. And now that it *had* happened, now that he had Chloe, he wanted it settled, wanted to seal the deal.

Okay, yeah. It had happened pretty fast with them. Some would say too fast.

But he didn't see it that way. They'd known each other since kindergarten. And besides, the way he looked at it, a thing either worked or it didn't. And what he and Chloe had together worked just fine. He wanted her at his side at the end of the workday—and in his bed every night.

She'd said yes. The decision was made. Why not take that walk down the aisle?

Chloe needed time, though. And he knew he had to give her that, had to keep a rein on his growing impatience to set the date and make her his bride, to blend their lives together in the fullest way, be husband and wife for the whole world to see.

Three and a half weeks had passed since the night she kicked her mother out of her house, the night she'd said she wanted to wait to set the date until after their engagement party—but then turned right around and insisted that she still wanted to get married soon.

Well, the engagement party had been and gone. She hadn't said word one since then about when they could stand up in front of a judge.

If she didn't bring it up soon, he would do it. And he had a strange intuition that it wouldn't go well.

Beside him, Chloe shifted slightly. Her fingers brushed

the back of his hand. Heat and longing shivered across his skin. He caught her hand and laced their fingers together, turning his gaze to her.

God, she was beautiful. She stared straight ahead at the altar, where Dalton Ames had just been told he could kiss his bride. A soft smile curved her mouth, a smile Quinn knew was just for him.

When she smiled like that, his worries vanished. What they had was so damn good. And it would only get better. He just had to choose the right moment to remind her that if she wanted the wedding to be soon, they needed to set the damn date.

The next day, Sunday, Chloe gave Annabelle her fairy princess costume, complete with featherweight, glittery lavender wings. Annabelle clapped her hands and jumped up and down with glee. Then she put on the costume and danced around the house, waving the matching wand in the air, tapping the chairs and tables, the sofa and the lampshades. Manny asked her, what, exactly, she was doing.

"Magic," she said, and whirled on to the kitchen.

"I think she's sprinkling fairy dust," Chloe explained. "You know, like Tinker Bell in *Peter Pan*?"

Manny, who was on his way out the door to spend the afternoon in Boulder with Doris, caught the fairy princess as she was dancing by and scooped her up into his arms. "Give me a hug and I'm outta here."

Annabelle tapped him lightly on the head with her wand. "There, Manny. Magic for you. Here's some for Granny Doris, too." She tapped him again. And then she wrapped her arms around his neck and squeezed good and tight.

"How 'bout some sugar?" He pointed at his grizzled cheek.

She planted a big smacker on him. "Now put me down. I'm very busy."

He let her go and she danced off up the stairs, spreading fairy dust as she went.

After Manny left, Chloe packed a picnic for the three of them. Annabelle begged to wear her fairy costume and neither Quinn nor Chloe could see why she shouldn't. Her rubber rain boots had purple flowers on them, and Annabelle decided they were perfect for a fairy princess, so she wore them with the dress. Chloe helped her remove the wings for the ride in the car.

They drove out to the national forest and parked a mile or so from a spot Chloe knew that had picnic tables. Annabelle put her wings back on—and off they went. As they strolled beneath the tall trees, Quinn and Chloe held hands, and Annabelle danced along beside them in her rubber boots and fairy princess dress, waving her magic wand, spreading fairy dust far and wide.

It was a great day. By eight that evening, when Chloe had kissed Annabelle good-night and gone back across the street to her house, Quinn was thinking that this was the night to bring up the wedding date. Manny should be home by ten to look after Annabelle. And Chloe would be expecting Quinn at her place. He would bring up the wedding first thing, before he took off all her clothes and buried himself in her softness.

So yeah, he was maybe a little preoccupied when he tucked Annabelle into bed. She chattered away about her fairy princess dress and how she planned to wear it in her princess bedroom as soon as Chloe finished "dec'rating" down the hill at the other house.

"I will be a fairy princess in my princess room, Daddy."

He smiled and nodded, tucking the covers in around

her and her teddy bear, thinking how she was bound to get princess overload soon and also half rehearsing how best to coax Chloe into settling on a wedding date.

"Daddy?"

"What, Annie-mo-manny?"

"Daddy." She caught his face between her little hands. "I'm not Manny. Look at me. Stop being silly."

He opened his mouth to tease her some more—and something in those big brown eyes stopped him. "Okay."

"I need to ask you…"

"Yeah? What?"

"Well, Daddy. Do you think my mommy would like my fairy princess dress?" She gazed up at him, so sweet and hopeful, her shining brown hair spread across her butterfly-printed pillow.

"I, uh…" His voice had a cracked sound to it and the spit seemed to have dried right up in his mouth. He swallowed hard to get the damn saliva going again and managed, "I think your mommy would love it."

"Can she come to see me, please? I need to show her my fairy princess dress and my wings and my magic wand."

His mind went dead blank, the way it used to do way back in elementary school when he would open a schoolbook and stare down at the incomprehensible chains of letters jittering across the page.

Yeah. Just like being a kid again, his brain refusing to function, his heart like a damn wrecking ball, swinging hard, battering the cage of his chest.

He wanted to leap up and run downstairs and across the street, to drag Chloe back over here, have her handle this. Please God, he really didn't want to blow it.

Annabelle continued to gaze up at him, trusting, serious—and waiting for his answer.

Suddenly he could almost hear Chloe's voice in his mind. *Answer her question as simply as possible.* "No, baby. Your mommy can't come."

"Why?"

His throat locked up tight. But he didn't give up. He squeezed the words right through the tightness. "Because when you were born, she gave you to me. She trusted me to love you and take care of you."

"And then she went away?"

"Yeah. Then she went away."

"Why?"

He realized he hated that question. "She…had a lot of things to do."

"What things?"

"Baby, I don't really know. I only know that she gave you to me to take care of and I am so glad that she did."

"She won't come back, ever?"

"No, I don't think she will. And that's why you have Manny and me, because we love you so much."

"And you like to take care of me?"

"Oh, yeah. We love to take care of you."

Annabelle fingered her old blanket. She had her scruffy teddy bear in a headlock. "Does Chloe like to take care of me?"

He tried a smile, though it probably looked more like a grimace, he was so freaked that he might be royally screwing this up. "Yes, she does."

"Well, then, Daddy. I think it's very good that we have Chloe now."

It damn well was good. And having his first real talk with his daughter about her missing mother had slammed it forcefully home to him: he wasn't the only one who would suffer if this thing with Chloe went south.

Not that it would. They were solid, him and Chloe...

"Daddy?"

"Yeah, baby."

"I love you, Daddy."

His heart seemed to blow up like a hot air balloon, filling his chest, rising into his throat so he had to gulp hard before he could answer her. "And I love you. So much."

She gave him her most beautiful, glowing smile—and hit him up. "So...can I have a puppy, then? Please?"

For once, he felt only relief that she was working him. Because if she was working him, that meant she was okay. It meant that the talk about her mother had gone pretty well. He leaned closer, until their noses touched. And then he whispered, "Nice try."

Damned if she didn't bat her eyelashes at him. "Puh-leeeaasse, Daddy?"

He was seriously tempted to just tell her no. But he and Manny were still considering the puppy issue. If he told her no and changed his mind later, she'd only become more adorably impossible, more certain that the word *no* only meant *Keep pushing and the grown-ups will give in.*

She kept after him. "Please, Daddy. A puppy would be so good. Or maybe a little bitty kitten."

He finally spoke up. "Do you want me to say no?"

"Daddy." The big eyes reproached him now. "You know what I want. I want you to say yes, and then I can have a puppy."

"Well, I'm not going to say yes. I'm going to say goodnight. Or no. You get to choose."

"But—"

He put his finger to her lips. "Choose."

"Daddy," she scolded, as though *he* was trying to put one over on *her.* And then she blew out a big sigh that smelled of Bubble Mint toothpaste. "You can say good-night."

He kissed her forehead and gave the covers one more good tuck nice and tight around her and the old bear. "Good night, baby."

She murmured, "Night, Daddy," as he stepped into the hall and shut the door.

At her house, Chloe got to work updating Your Way's website and adding and scheduling posts to the Your Way Facebook page.

It was about time. She'd been seriously neglecting Your Way's online presence. Given a choice between posting decorating tips and picnicking with Quinn and fairy princess Annabelle... Well, what kind of choice was that?

Quinn and Annabelle won, hands down.

Once she had the website spruced up a bit with new content, as well as seven new posts written and sched-uled to pop up on the Facebook page daily for the next week, she got to work plowing through email for both email accounts, the one for the website and the one she used for Facebook.

She did the website mail first. There were twenty emails left after purging junk and spam. She tackled them by date, oldest first. The fifth one down was no address she recognized, flwrs4yoo@gotmail.com. The subject line read Question for you.

Should that have alerted her?

It didn't. She assumed it was just someone wanting decorating advice or information about her services.

She so didn't pick up the meaning. She had no clue, just blithely pointed the mouse at the thing and started reading.

Did you like the flowers? I've been waiting to hear from you. We had so much, we had it all. I know you remember. Nothing's right anymore. I can't stop thinking about you.
Ted

Chapter Ten

For a moment, Chloe just stared at the monitor, unblinking and unbelieving. Then she shoved back her chair, ran to the downstairs bath and stood there before the mirror, staring at her too-pale stricken face, not quite sure if she might be about to throw up or not.

Finally, when she felt reasonably certain her dinner wasn't coming up, she went upstairs, poured herself a tall glass of water and drank it down. After that, still shaking, feeling hollow and powerless, vibrating with anger, she went back down to her office and tried to decide what to do next.

Twenty minutes later, she'd trashed and retrieved that damn email five times. She'd composed several replies, all along the lines of *I want nothing to do with you. Do not contact me again.*

In the end, she didn't reply. Any response would only encourage him. How many times had she told him to leave her alone? Too many. It did zero good. She considered blocking the address, but decided against that. If he sent more, she wanted to know about it, wanted to know if he was escalating.

She saved the email itself to a folder that she named TD. Then she wrote a brief description of the flowers and the note he'd sent all those weeks ago. She wrote that she'd thrown the flowers, vase and note in the trash and she marked the date that the incident had occurred. She added that information to the folder, as well.

Okay, it wasn't much. Not enough to get the police interested. But if he kept it up, so would she. From now on, she would have a record of every move he made.

By then, at least, she wasn't shaking. Tomorrow night was the third meeting of her self-defense class. She was on this case, taking responsibility to deal with whatever went down. If she had to confront Ted again, she would be better prepared than she'd been in the past.

She scanned the rest of the website emails and then the messages to Your Way's Facebook page and her own personal timeline page. As far as she could tell, he hadn't tried to contact her again. She decided to consider that reassuring.

She thought about Quinn, pictured his beloved face, the heat of him, the strength and goodness. Instantly, the tears were pressing at the back of her throat. She wanted to feel his arms around her, wanted to tell him everything, about the email, about her decision to keep a record of any and every move her ex made on her.

But then she remembered that look in his eyes the night she'd told him about the flowers. She'd barely been able to get his word then that he would stay out of it.

If she told him about the email, would she manage to get his agreement to stay out of it now?

She knew the answer. Because she knew him.

Really, it was only an email. Only one tiny step along a possible road to another ugly confrontation with the awful man she'd had the bad judgment to marry.

Eventually, if Ted kept it up, she would have to tell Quinn, have to somehow convince him again that this was *her* problem to solve in her own way. When that happened, Quinn would not be happy with her that she'd kept the truth from him now.

But Ted hadn't tried again in the past two weeks. She didn't *have* to tell Quinn now. And she wouldn't. It wasn't his problem and she could deal with this herself.

Downstairs after tucking Annabelle in, Quinn had stretched out on the couch and started *The Great Gatsby* on audio book, expecting his daughter to reappear any minute for their nightly exercise in monster removal. She never came. Bouncing around all day in rubber boots and fairy wings must have worn her out.

When Manny got home, Quinn took five minutes to run down his bedtime conversation with Annabelle, just to keep the old man in the loop on the mommy questions and the ongoing puppy issue. Then he said good-night and headed across the street to Chloe's.

They'd traded keys weeks ago, so he let himself in and dealt with the alarm. She'd left a lamp on by the sofa, as she always did. He could hear the low drone of a television, and light glowed from the short hallway that led to the master suite. Then the TV went silent. She must have heard him come in.

A second later, wearing the same big pink shirt she'd worn the first night he came to her, she appeared in the door to the short hall that led to the bedroom. "Hey." Her sweet mouth trembled slightly. And there was something in her eyes, something that looked a lot like fear.

"What's wrong?"

"Nothing," she said too fast. "I just…heard the door, you know? Came to check…"

"Check what?"

She shivered, though the house wasn't cold. "Nothing. Really." She tipped her head toward the bedroom. "Come on." And then she turned and disappeared back the way she'd come.

Something here was very far from right.

He followed her to the bedroom and found her already in the bed, propped against the pillows. She patted the space beside her.

But he hesitated in the doorway as he tried to figure out what the hell was going on with her. "What's happened?"

"Nothing." Breathless. And lying.

He left the doorway. Her eyes were anxious as she watched him come to her.

Instead of going around to what had pretty much become his side of the bed, he went straight for her. She scooted aside a little to make room. He sat on the edge of the mattress.

She stared at him. He watched her satiny throat move as she swallowed. "What?" she asked finally. "Honestly there's…" She faltered and then seemed not to have the heart to go on.

"See?" he said gently. "You don't want to lie to me, not really." He reached out and speared his fingers in her long, shining hair. He wrapped a thick golden hank of the stuff around his hand and pulled her face right up to his. "I know you, angel," he whispered against her satiny lips. "Know you better every day, every hour, every minute we're together. You're getting inside me, like I'm in you. It's getting so that it only takes me one look in your beautiful face, and I know if things aren't right with you. So I'll say it again. Something is wrong and I want you to tell me what it is."

Her glance shifted away. "Would you let go of me, please?"

He did what she asked instantly, unwinding her sweet-smelling hair from around his fist, sliding his fingers free. "Done." He stood.

She gazed up at him, her eyes like a stormy sea. "You're angry."

He shook his head. And then he turned for the door, more afraid with every step that she was going to let him go.

But she was better than that. "Please, Quinn. Don't go."

He stopped in the doorway and faced her again. "*Is* something wrong?"

She had her arms wrapped around herself, her shoulders curved in protectively. For a moment, she mangled her lower lip between her pretty white teeth. And then, at last, she confessed, "Yes." Once the single word escaped her, she yanked her shoulders back and glared at him. "And if I tell you, you have to respect my wishes. You can't go taking matters into your own hands. I need your word on that, Quinn."

Not her mother, then. The douche canoe ex. Had to be. "Just tell me."

Her delicate jaw was set. "Not until you promise."

He could see it so clearly and it would be beautiful. Just him, the ex and maybe a fat length of steel pipe, up close and personal—and hold on a minute. No. Scratch the pipe. Much more satisfying to deliver the message with his bare fists.

"I mean it, Quinn. You have to promise me."

He studied her unforgettable face for several really

long seconds. No doubt about it. She meant what she said. Plus, a man had to respect the wishes of his woman. He made himself release the pleasant fantasy of teaching Ted Davies a lesson in pain he would never forget. "All right. You have my word. Anything I do, you'll agree to it first."

She watched him narrow-eyed. "Is that a trick answer?"

"Come on. You know me. If I give my word, you can count on it."

Her slim shoulders sagged again. She shut her eyes, drew in a slow breath and when she looked at him once more, she held out her hand. "Please come back."

He couldn't get to her fast enough. He took the hand she offered and dropped down beside her. "I'm here. I'm listening."

She let out a small, sad little sound low in her throat.

That got to him, made an ache in him, the deep-down kind. He hated it when she was sad. He slid his other hand along her soft cheek and then wrapped it around the nape of her neck, beneath the heavy fall of her hair. He pulled her close.

She settled against him, feeling like heaven in his arms, smelling of French soap and fancy flowers he didn't even know the names of. He caught her face between his hands and tipped it up to brush a kiss across those lips he never tired of tasting. "It's okay," he promised, stroking a hand down her hair. "It's going to be okay…" Because he would damn well make it so. He kissed her again.

She clung to him for a minute and then pulled back and settled against the pillows. "I was checking the emails for the Your Way website," she began. And she went on to tell him about the message Davies had sent her and the file she'd started on him. When she was done, she added hopefully, "It was only one email and he sent it two weeks ago. I hadn't gotten around to checking the website in a while. Nothing since then. I really don't think it's that big a deal."

He disagreed, though he didn't say so. It *was* a big deal. The dirtbag refused to leave her alone—after all this time, after she'd pulled up stakes and moved home to get away from him. He said, "You need to write back to him."

She was shaking her head before he could finish the sentence. "That never works. You have no idea how many times I've told him I want nothing to do with him ever again."

"But you're keeping a record now, remember? It's been more than a year since you left San Diego. Unless you have a restraining order on him or some formal proof somewhere that he's harassed you in the past...?"

"No," she admitted unhappily. "God. I was such a big coward."

He took her by the shoulders. "Look at me."

"Oh, Quinn..."

"Listen. This is not your fault. You are not to blame here. This guy is a major scumball and *he's* the one who's causing the trouble. Guys like that, they love to make you think it's all somehow your fault. Don't you fall for that garbage. Don't you let him do that to you."

She pressed her lips together and nodded. "You're right. I know you're right."

"Good." He gave her shoulders a last squeeze and let her go. "So you write a two-sentence email. 'Never contact me again. I am blocking this email address.' And you send it to him. You forward his email and your reply to me and then you block him."

She stiffened against the pillows. "Wait a minute. Why am I forwarding it on to you?"

"I'm going to write to Ted and introduce myself."

"Oh, no. No, now, that is a bad idea…"

"Don't give me that look. There's nothing to get freaked out about. There'll be no dirty words and I won't be making any threats. Just a simple, straight-up little note. I'm going to tell him that I'm your fiancé and I know you've blocked him and told him you don't want to hear from him again. Ever. I'll say that I expect him to respect your wishes and if he has questions, he should write back to me, that I'll be happy to deal with anything he has to say." Her eyes were mutinous. He could see her quick brain working, ticking off objections. He went on. "You can read it before I send it—in fact, emails aren't really my strong suit. Takes me forever to write one. So I'll bring my tablet over tomorrow night. I'll dictate the email to you and you can type it in for me, so you'll know exactly what I'm sending. Then that can go in your file, too."

"But…what if he writes back to you?"

"Oh, angel. I hope he does."

"Quinn. I don't like this. The whole point is that I don't want you involved."

"How can I not be involved? We're getting married, remember?" *If I can ever get you to set the damn date.*

"It's not that. It's not about us. It's my old…*stuff*, you know? My big, ugly mess. I should be the one dealing with it."

He reached for her then and pulled her close. She resisted at first, but then she sagged against him with a long sigh. He wrapped his arms good and tight around her and reminded her, "You *are* dealing with it. You can't get away from it. Look at you. It's tearing you up inside. I'm only backup, that's all. I only want this jerk to know that you're not alone, that you got family and we got your back."

She cuddled in closer. "When you say it that way, I almost feel justified in dragging you into this."

He pressed his lips into her hair. "You're not dragging me. I'm a gung-ho volunteer."

She gave a weary little laugh and then grew serious again as she tipped her head back to meet his eyes. "Any communication you get from him, I have to read, Quinn. You don't get to protect me from anything he says. And I want to read it right away. No putting off sharing it with me while you decide on your own what to do next. You bring it to me. We decide together."

A few bad words scrolled through his head. He'd hoped to have a little more leeway. But at least she'd agreed to the basic plan. "All right. He writes back, I bring it to you, we decide together what to do next."

She lifted herself up and kissed him. "Agreed." She breathed the words against his mouth. Her soft breasts pressed into his chest.

He wanted to kiss her some more, to take off that pink shirt, to see if she had anything else on under it and get rid of that, too. But they weren't finished with the subject of Ted. "There's more."

She moaned. "Oh, God. What else?"

"Do you remember what florist those flowers came from?"

"Bloom. Why?"

He'd figured as much. There were only two florists in town. His sister Jody owned Bloom. Jody had a real flair. Tilly's Flowers, at the other end of Central from Bloom, was kind of boring by comparison. "You call Jody tomorrow and you get her to look up the order for the flowers he sent you. Then you ask her not to accept any more orders from Ted."

"What if the order came from some big online company and Jody only filled it?"

He bent close, nibbled on her ear and whispered, "Jody will know how to refuse any more orders from him, believe me."

"So, then, if he does it again, he'll just use Tilly's."

"And then you'll block him from Tilly's. After that, he'd have to get them delivered from Boulder. All I'm saying is, why make it easy for him? Not to mention, Jody can send you a copy of the original order and of the note that came with the flowers, meaning you'll have proof that he sent them."

"Hmm. Well, proof would be good…"

He studied her worried face. "You're still not on board with this. Why?"

She reached up and pressed her soft hand to his cheek. "I'm ashamed to admit it…"

"You got nothing—*nothing*—to be ashamed of."

"Yes, I do. In the end, I'm my mother's daughter through and through. I don't want to call Jody because I'm worried about what your sister's going to think of me." He probably shouldn't have grinned at that, but he did. And she shoved at his shoulder. "Don't you laugh at me."

"I'm not laughing, and you're worried about nothing. I can tell you what my sister's gonna think."

"Oh, really?" She kind of looked a little like her mother right then, one eyebrow raised, all superior and cool—not that he was fool enough to tell her that. "Now you read minds?"

He shrugged. "Jody will think that you're engaged to me and you don't want flowers from other guys."

She blinked. "Oh. Well. That's a good point. She probably will think that. *I* would think that."

"Damn straight." He bent close and nuzzled her throat. God, she always smelled so good.

She wrapped her hand around the back of his head, threading her soft fingers into his hair. "Come to bed now," she whispered.

He kissed her once, hard and fast. "We're not done here."

She groaned. "I can tell by the look in your eyes. I'm not going to like whatever it is you're going to say next."

"Probably not. You need to call your mother. We need to have a talk with her."

"Quinn! How can you say that? I'm not speaking to my mother."

"Yeah, you are. At least long enough to get what we can out of her. You said she's been in touch with Davies."

"Which is why I don't want to talk to her. She betrayed me."

"Chloe. Think about it. We need to know exactly what she's told him—and what *he's* said to *her.*"

"That's assuming she'll answer a single question we ask her."

"We need to try."

"No. Really, I don't want anything to do with her. Everything else will be plenty, *more* than plenty."

He ran a finger down the side of her throat. Smooth as satin, every inch of her skin—and he needed to keep on task here. He explained, "So far, Ted's the aggressor. Always has been. So far, the way it's always been, *he* chases *you.* You see that, right? You see that has to change."

"But I don't want to chase him or *aggress* on him. I just want to be finished with him, to have him completely out of my life."

"Yeah, well, Chloe, sometimes the only way to get rid of a problem is to make yourself ready to stand up against it. So if the time ever comes when you have to go toe-to-toe, you're in the light."

"What does that mean, the light?"

"It means that whatever you can learn about your opponent, you learn. You don't hide from the facts. You don't lie to yourself. You don't go brushing things under carpets and worrying about what other people are gonna think. You admit your own weaknesses and work to get stronger. You never deny his strengths or refuse to admit how far he might go. You bring everything out in the open. Into the light."

She dipped her head close and rested against his shoulder. In a small voice, she asked, "My mother? Really?"

He tipped up her chin to him. "You can call her in the morning."

"Ugh."

"You watch. It's going to be fine."

"Keep telling me that."

He gathered the fabric of her big shirt in his two fists. "Right now I got other things on my mind. Lift up your arms."

Grateful that they were finally through discussing what to do about Ted, Chloe lifted her arms. Quinn took her pink shirt up and away.

"Come here." She tried to reach for him again.

"Wait." He got up, but only to pull back the covers. "What's this?" His eyes had that gleam in them. And the look on his face sent heat surging through her.

"Tap pants."

"Pretty." He bent close and ran a slow finger along the lace band that crossed her stomach just below her navel. Goose bumps chased themselves across her skin, and longing pounded in her veins with every hungry beat of her heart. He eased the tap pants down and tossed them over his shoulder.

By the time he rose to his height and yanked his T-shirt over his head, she'd all but forgotten about her mother, about Ted, about the unpleasant things she needed to do in the morning to bring the situation "into the light," as he called it.

For now, for the rest of the night, there was only Quinn. Only this beauty they had between them, only the feel of his hands on her yearning flesh, the deep rumble of his voice filling her head. Only her need to be with him, held by him, filled so full of him that there was only her love for him and the hope and joy he brought her, day by day.

Naked, he came down to her. She wrapped her arms around him, breathing in the clean, male scent of him, loving the feel of him under her hands. He rolled them until he was on his side of the bed, on his back, with her on top. With a gasp and a short burst of laughter at the suddenness of the move, she gazed down at him. Such a beautiful man, inside and out.

"What?" he asked, gathering her hair and lifting it, wrapping it around his arm the way he loved to do. "You don't want to be on top?"

Any way he wanted it was fine with her. "I'll be on top." She bent and pressed her mouth to his. "On top is perfect." Even better because they didn't have to fumble for condoms anymore, not since the talk they'd had a couple of weeks before. She'd been on the pill for months, long before the first time he came up the hill to her. As for safety, well, there'd been no one for her since her divorce. For him, it had been over a year. And since that slipup that became Annabelle, he'd never gone without protection.

More kisses, deep and wet and never-ending. He unwound her hair and smoothed it back over her shoulder. It only fell forward again, curling between them, tangling around them.

He caressed her with long, lovely strokes. She rose up to her knees above him as he touched her, his big hands moving down her body, cupping her breasts, rolling her nipples between his thumbs and forefingers. When he found the heart of her, she cried out. He answered with a low groan of satisfaction as he dipped inside and, oh, she was so wet and so ready.

She couldn't wait any longer. She reached down and wrapped her eager fingers around the thick, hard length of him. The sound that escaped him then was like a groan of pain.

But it wasn't pain. It was pure pleasure. She guided him into her and sank slowly down, taking him deep and then deeper still. He surged up, meeting her, filling her all the way, until she let her head drop back and gave herself up to him.

The only word in her mouth was his name, the only thought in her head was of him, of the two of them, together, with nothing between them but heat and wonder and the slow, thick pulse of their shared pleasure, their mutual desire.

He came first, his big hands at either side of her waist, holding her down, tight to him, hard. She felt him pulsing and that sent her over, too.

In the end, she collapsed on top of him. He wrapped her up close in those muscled, inked arms of his. And he brushed kisses against her cheek. He breathed them into her tangled hair, laid them in a sweet, hot line along the curve of her shoulder.

A little while later, before they went to sleep, he told her about his bedtime conversation with Annabelle.

When he finished, his sea-green eyes full of fatherly doubt, he asked, "You think I did okay?"

"You did beautifully. Just right."

He grunted. "But I'm not out of the woods on the subject of Annabelle's mom yet, am I?"

"Truth?" she asked.

"Yeah."

"The good news is you've told Annabelle what she needs to hear for now. She probably won't bring it up again for months, maybe years."

"But she *will* bring it up again. That's what you're tellin' me, right?"

"Almost certainly, yes."

"Crap."

"Lighten up, Quinn. It's human nature to want to understand where we came from."

"Yeah. Okay. I know you're right."

"I *am* right—about this, anyway. And you really are a good dad."

"Yeah?"

"Absolutely. You love her. She knows it. She's a happy little girl. That's what matters. The rest, you'll work out as you go along." She turned to glance at the bedside clock. After midnight. "Let's get some sleep." She sat up and turned to reach for the switch.

He touched her shoulder. "Chloe…" His voice was hesitant now. Careful.

She dropped her arm and focused on him. "Now what?" She said it teasingly, with a silly eye roll and a breathy laugh.

But he wasn't laughing. Far from it. He stared at her, a burning kind of look, his eyes gone dark as night. "I want to set the date. I want us to be married. And soon, like you said when you told me yes. I want you living in my house. Or we can buy another house that you like better. Anything you want. It doesn't matter where we live. It matters that we belong to each other and that the whole world knows that we do."

Chapter Eleven

"I..." Chloe had nothing.

It was getting to be a habit with her. Quinn brought up setting the date, and instantly her mind was a muddy swirl of all the stuff she hadn't worked through yet, of Ted and her mother, all the leftover threads of her old, screwed-up life that kept popping back up to remind her of her mistakes, her questionable choices, her longtime fear of facing hard truths.

Quinn's gaze burned right through her. And then he echoed her. "'I...'? One little word. That's it? That's all you got?"

It wasn't all. Not by a long shot. There was so much. Starting with *I love you*. She desperately needed to tell him that. But she just didn't feel she had the right yet. She wanted to be good for him, someone who made his life better, not someone who dragged him down. "There's so much going on."

His full mouth became a hard line. He wasn't falling for her excuses. "Lame, Chloe. You're better than this."

"But that's just the thing…"

"What's the thing?"

What if I'm not better? What if I'm not all you think I am, Quinn?

What if she never really got beyond the stupid choices she'd made in the past? What if he married her and ended up wishing he hadn't?

She had all these horrible doubts about herself. But *he* didn't doubt her. He believed in her, so completely. In a way that no one else ever had.

Somehow she needed to prove herself, needed to be certain that she wouldn't end up letting him down. But how to do that? She didn't have a clue.

"Nothin', huh?" His voice betrayed his disappointment, but his expression had softened. "Go ahead. Turn off the light." He said the words so gently, giving in for now, letting her off the hook once again.

She knew she should do better, say something meaningful and true. But what? He was right. Right now she had nothing more to offer him on this subject, and they both knew it.

So she switched off the lamp—and then didn't have the nerve to cuddle back against him. Instead, she rolled onto her side, facing away from him. Wrapping the covers close again, she clung miserably to her edge of the bed.

His wonderful voice came out of the dark, all rough and low and grumbly. "Come here." He reached out and hauled her back against him.

Shamelessly, she snuggled in tight. She felt his warm breath stir her hair. Safe in his strong arms, she closed her eyes.

* * *

When she woke in the morning, Quinn had already left. She turned off her alarm before it could start chiming and lay back on her pillow and pictured him across the street, sharing breakfast with Annabelle and Manny. She wished she were there with them.

And she *could* be there, living in his house with him, never again having to wake up and slide her hand across the sheet to the cool, empty space on his side of the bed. Even if she wasn't ready to say "I do" yet, he would agree to her moving in if she asked him.

But somehow that didn't feel right, either. When she moved in, it really should be forever, for everyone's sake. And she wasn't ready for forever.

Chloe showered and dressed for work. Before she ate breakfast, she called her mother. No way could she eat anything with that call ahead of her.

Her mother answered on the second ring. "Chloe? This *is* a surprise." Linda's tone was etched in acid.

Chloe ignored the sudden knot in her stomach and got right to the point. "Will you come here, to my house, tomorrow night at seven? I have a few things I'd like to clear up with you."

"What things?"

"We'll talk about them when you get here."

"I don't like your tone, Chloe. I don't like any of this. I don't understand what's *happened* to you. Your father told me that you're engaged to Quinn Bravo—not that he *had* to tell me. Everyone in town knows. Everyone is talking." She started firing off angry questions, not even bothering to pause for Chloe to answer. "Have you lost your mind? What's the matter with you? This insanity is not like you. Are you going through some kind of life crisis?" She stopped for a breath at last.

And Chloe spoke up before she could get rolling again. "Seven tomorrow night. Yes or no?"

A long, nerve-racking silence and then, more softly, almost hopefully: "Yes. All right. I'll be there."

"Good. I'll see you then." Chloe hung up.

She had two cups of coffee and some toast and then went to work. Tai came in at ten that day. It was her first day as a full-time Your Way employee. She'd decided to go to a few online classes for at least a semester and then reevaluate whether to return to CU or not. It was a stretch budgetwise for Chloe, but Tai was willing to take minimum wage for a while, and her presence would free Chloe up to spend more time designing and working with clients. As soon as Tai arrived, Chloe let her handle the showroom and went to the small office room in back to call Bloom.

"Chloe!" Jody Bravo seemed happy to hear from her. "Hey. What can I do for you?"

"I…" Great. She was at it again. Doling out one-word sentences consisting of *I*.

"Chloe? You there? Everything all right?"

She started to lie, to chirp out a cheerful *Oh, yes. Everything's fine.*

But then she thought of all the years she'd told people things were fine when they were anything but. She thought of Quinn last night, telling her she needed to be "in the light."

"Chloe…?"

"Oh, Jody. I'm sorry. This is difficult for me."

"It's okay." Jody really seemed to mean it. "Honestly. Whatever it is, whatever I can do, I'm happy to help."

Chloe forged on. "A month ago you got an order for me. You sent me a beautiful arrangement. Orchids and roses in a gorgeous square vase?"

"Okay, yeah. I remember that. Do you recall the date?"

It was burned in Chloe's brain. She repeated it. Jody said, "Let me look… Got it. Came through FloraDora dot net. From a Ted Davies in San Diego."

"That's it." The truth was right there caught in her throat, pushing to get out. So she let it. "Ted Davies is my ex-husband and I don't want any more flowers from him."

"Whoa. I hear you." Computer keys clicked on the other end of the line. "Okay. That's handled. If I get another order from him, I'll refuse it."

"Thanks. Thanks so much. And one more thing…"

"Just ask."

"Do you have a copy of that order and maybe the text of the card that came with it?"

"I do."

"Could you email that to me?"

"The text of the card, absolutely. I can't send the actual order form. But I can send you a confirmation that I received and filled the order. A confirmation would include the date of the transaction and that Ted Davies in San Diego had the flowers sent to you."

"That would be perfect." Chloe rattled off her personal email address.

Jody said, "Great." More keys clacked. "I've sent what you asked for. And if he tries again, I'll let you know."

"That would really help."

"And, Chloe, just so you know…"

"Please."

"If he starts sending them anonymously from Tilly's or elsewhere, you'll probably get resistance from the florist when you ask for information about who sent them." Jody lowered her voice. "The customer is king and all that…"

"I understand. And I can't tell you how much I appreciate your help."

"Anytime. And, Chloe…?"

"Um?"

"Maybe it's none of my business, but…" Jody hesitated again.

Chloe felt a curl of dread that the conversation was about to veer way out of her comfort zone. But then again, Jody *was* Quinn's sister. And Chloe had already all but said that her ex was a stalker. Comfort zone? Forget about it. Chloe reminded Jody, "We're family, remember?" Or they would be, if Chloe ever agreed to choose a date. "Ask me anything."

"Does Quinn know about this?"

"Yes." It did feel good to be able to reassure his sister that she hadn't kept him in the dark. "Quinn's the one who suggested that I call you."

"Perfect." Jody's relief was clear in her voice. "Exactly what I wanted to hear. You need anything else—anything—you just let me know."

Chloe thanked her again and they said goodbye. She disconnected the call—and the phone rang in her hand.

It was Quinn. "Thought I'd check and see how you're doing."

Just the sound of his voice made her feel better about everything. She reported on her call to her mother and told him that everything was handled with Jody.

"Look at you," he said in that low rumble that turned her insides to mush. "Right on the case."

She chuckled. Okay, it was a slightly manic sound, but a laugh was better than a cry of misery and frustration anytime. "I'm in the light, big guy. Stalker Ted doesn't stand a chance against me."

"Get 'em, killer."

"You'd better be smiling when you call me that."

They talked for a little about mundane things.

She had her self-defense class that night and she was looking forward to more tips on eluding an attacker. Also, for the second half of that evening's class, the guys would finally get into their padded suits. She would have a chance to put some of what she'd learned into practice.

Quinn said that he and Annabelle would miss her at dinner. "Manny's making lasagna," he muttered bleakly.

She teased, "I'm so sorry about that."

Tai appeared in the open doorway to the showroom. A customer wanted an estimate for both a bath and a kitchen remodeling.

Quinn said, "I heard that. See you tonight. I'll be over as soon as I finish with monster removal."

Chloe left her self-defense class that night feeling exhilarated. At first, it was scary, shouting at her "attacker," kicking and flailing, punching and pushing to get out of his clutches, trying to remember the few fighting tricks she'd been taught in earlier classes, like how to behave counter to your natural reaction to jerk away when an attacker grabbed you. Instead, you leaned in, catching him off balance, and then, using that split second when the bad guy wasn't braced, you jerked back and started kicking and screaming for all you were worth.

Bottom line: it didn't pay to be a lady when some scuzzball grabbed you. Once things moved past avoidance and any chance to defuse the situation, a woman needed to be willing to make plenty of noise and fight tooth and nail for all she was worth. She had to accept that she would probably be injured. The battle by then was to survive.

When she got home, she took a long shower and put on cropped jeans and a silk tank top and fixed a light dinner. By then, it was nine and Quinn would be over sometime in the next hour. She went downstairs and checked email, her pulse ratcheting up a notch at the thought that Ted might have tried to contact her again.

But there was nothing from him. Jody had sent her a copy of the note that had come with the flowers, along with the confirmation she'd promised. Chloe copied all that to her TD file. Then she dealt with the few new emails and messages the website and the Facebook page had received.

Finally, she brought up the message Ted had sent her two weeks ago. She and Quinn had agreed that she would answer with a demand that Ted leave her alone and then block the address. She went ahead and composed her reply. It was only two sentences: Never contact me again. I am blocking this address. She zipped it right off, blacklisted flwrs4yoo@gotmail.com and updated the information in her TD file.

Not two seconds later, she heard the door open upstairs.

"Angel?" Quinn called.

"Coming!" She ran up to meet him.

"So, how was the lasagna?" she asked when they met in the middle of the stairs.

He had his tablet in one hand. With the other, he reached out, slid his warm fingers around the back of her neck and pulled her up close. "About as expected."

"That's too bad."

"Yeah." He leaned in even closer, rubbed his rough cheek to her soft one. "You shoulda been there to suffer with us."

"So sorry to miss it."

"I'll just bet you are."

She rubbed her nose against his and then kissed him. When he lifted his head, she stared up at him, feeling distinctly starry-eyed. "How 'bout a beer?" she suggested. "We can sit out on the deck and I'll tell you all about how spectacular the master bath tile work at your house is going to be and what I learned in self-defense class this evening."

He held up his tablet. "First, you're writing me an email to Ted, remember?"

She hadn't forgotten. Far from it. "Actually, I've been rethinking that."

He guided a hank of her hair behind her ear and chided, "We got this all worked out. It's only going to take a few minutes."

Dear Lord, he was a wonderful man. "I've done everything you suggested last night. I'm even going to deal with my mother tomorrow. And I want you to be here when she arrives. But this…" She gestured weakly at the tablet.

"What about it?" He didn't sound happy.

Well, neither was she. "I don't like it, Quinn."

"We've been all through this last night and you agreed—"

She cut him off—but gently. "Yes, I did. And since then, I've had time to think it over a little more and I just…"

"You just what?"

"I just don't want you contacting him. You are not getting directly involved in this—not with Ted. Uh-uh. That is not going to happen."

His eyes had darkened and now his jaw was solid as rock. "You better tell me right now. You think you need to protect that guy from me?"

She gaped in hurt surprise. "No. No, of course I don't. This is about you, not him. This is about—"

"So you're protecting *me*? You think I need protecting from a slimeball like that?"

How had this gotten so out of hand so fast? She drew in a slow breath and told her racing heart to settle the heck down. "Please. Can we dial this back? Can we *not* have this argument right here in the middle of the stairs?"

He answered much too quietly, "Sure, Chloe. Where, then?"

"How about if we just don't have this argument at all?"

He was not about to let it go. "*Where*, Chloe?"

Fair enough. She gestured toward the top of the stairs. "The great room, then."

He turned around and marched back up. Reluctantly, she followed.

In the sitting area, he took an easy chair and she took the sofa. They faced off across the coffee table.

He asked, oh so reasonably, "Did you write that sucker an email and tell him to leave you alone?"

"Yes, I did. And then I blocked the address he used."

"Good." He dropped his tablet on the coffee table and leaned toward her, powerful forearms braced on his spread knees. "So, what's the sudden issue with letting him know that you're with me now and I know what he's up to?"

"It's an overreaction."

"The hell it is."

"Flowers, Quinn. He sent flowers once, a month ago. And he emailed me two weeks ago. That's all he's done."

He made a low, angry sound deep in his throat. "All he's done? He hit you, more than once. He cheated on you. And then when you divorced him, he wouldn't leave you alone. It got so bad you moved back home. And now he's started in again."

"I'm talking about recently."

"You're lying to yourself."

"Two times," she repeated. "Two times he's contacted me in more than a year. Flowers and one email. And now I'm keeping a record of every move he makes on me. I've blocked his email address and he won't be sending me flowers from Bloom again. I've told him, in no uncertain terms, to get lost. That's enough for now. That's... appropriate to the situation."

"Appropriate." He said it as if it tasted really bad in his mouth. "Tell you what. Forget it. Let's drop this right now. Have it your way. Let it go."

"Great. All I need is your word that you won't be looking him up online or calling some private investigator to find him. Promise me you won't go off on your own and contact him."

"I'm not agreeing to that."

"Then we're not done here. I mean it, Quinn. You have to stay out of this. Ted is not your problem."

"You keep saying that." He sat back, then forward again. She saw the born fighter in him so clearly right then. Testosterone seemed to come off him in waves. "Ted *is* my problem." He growled the words. "Anything that ties you in knots and keeps you awake nights and drives a wedge between us..." He jerked his thumb toward his broad chest. "My problem."

She folded her arms protectively across her middle, realized she was doing it, and unfolded them again. "Ted is... He can be a real snake, Quinn." Across the low table from her, he shifted again, furious, coiled, ready for action. She went on before he could interrupt. "He's a really good lawyer. Clever. Ruthless. You get in touch with him, you could end up slapped with a restraining order, or even a lawsuit."

Quinn shot to his feet, the move lightning-fast. He was sitting across from her—and all at once, he was looming above her. But when he spoke his voice was careful and even. "You think I give a good damn about his dirty tricks?"

She answered truthfully, "No, I don't. But *I* do. I care

if he makes trouble for you. I will not be the cause of that. I just won't."

"You won't be the cause of anything. Your ex, *he's* the cause. And I'm responsible for my own actions. It's not on you if I communicate with Ted. So whatever he tries on me, fine. He can bring it."

Where to even start? "Will you please just…sit down?"

He surprised her by doing what she asked, dropping back into the chair and leaning forward on his spread knees again. "I told you last night that I'm not going to be anything but polite and respectful to that piece of crap."

"You're missing the point. I'll say it again. This is *my* problem and you don't get to solve it. I don't want you to solve it. That wouldn't be right."

"Yeah, it *is* right. You're with me and I stand up for what's mine."

"No, Quinn."

"Wait." His eyes burned into hers. "Now you're telling me you're not mine?"

So strange. Such fury in him right now—and yet she wasn't in the least afraid of him. She knew he would never hurt her, never lay a finger on her in anger, that all he wanted was to protect her.

But in this particular situation, she couldn't let him do that.

"Are you mine or not?" he demanded again.

And she gave him a slow, very definite nod. "I am yours, Quinn. Yes. Absolutely."

Heat flared in his eyes and he said, low and evenly, "Give me that email address."

"No."

"Damn it, Chloe."

"Don't swear at me. Listen. I don't feel I have to protect you from Ted and I certainly don't feel I have to protect him from anything. I am with you and only you. You're the one for me. I want your help. I want your strength and your support and I'm grateful for your advice. What I don't want is you standing up *for* me. The whole point here is that I have to learn how to stand up for myself."

He seemed unable to stay in the chair then. Shooting upright again, he glared down at her. "I don't like it. That guy needs to know you got backup, that you're not alone and the man you're with now will fight for you."

"It's my choice, Quinn. Tell me that you will respect my choice. Please."

"Angel, you ask too much."

"Please."

He turned from her, went to the wall of windows and stood staring out, feet apart, hands linked behind him. She resisted the powerful need to plead with him some more. Finally, he said, "I don't like it."

"I get that. It's painfully clear."

He faced her again. "Do I still have your word that you'll tell me if he sends you more flowers or tries in any way to get in touch with you again?"

"Yes."

"Then all right. I won't contact him. Until he makes some other jackass move, I'll stand down."

Chapter Twelve

After Quinn agreed not to contact Ted, the night went on pretty much as usual. They sat out on the deck under the clear night sky. They made beautiful, passionate love.

But it wasn't the same, not really. Except for their love-making, which was as intense and ardent as ever, something was missing. There was a certain edge between them. A certain distance.

Chloe hated that distance. But what could she do? No way would she give him her blessing to get into it with Ted.

The next evening, he came over at six-thirty. In the half hour before her mother's arrival, Chloe reminded him that she was running this little talk. He was there to lend support.

He didn't even argue. "I get that. No problem."

His immediate acceptance of her terms surprised her a little after how hard he'd fought her on the issue of his contacting Ted.

And he knew it, too.

He said wryly, "No worries. I don't want to give your mom a bad time. She's going to be my mother-in-law, remember? Eventually I'm hoping she and I can get along together."

"Have you *met* my mother?"

He chuckled then, an easy sound. She dared to hope that maybe they were getting past their disagreement of the night before.

The doorbell rang right at seven.

Chloe opened the door. Her mother stood there in tan trousers, a cream-colored silk blouse and the triple strand of Mikimoto pearls Chloe's dad had bought her for their thirtieth anniversary four years ago.

"Chloe," Linda said with a cool nod.

"Mom." She stepped back. "Come in."

Linda spotted Quinn as she crossed the threshold. She put her hand to her pearls and arched an eyebrow at Chloe. "I didn't realize *he* would be here."

Quinn moved closer. He didn't seem the least offended by her mother's snotty tone. "Good to see you, Mrs. Winchester."

Her mother blinked at his outstretched hand as though she feared it would bite. But then she gave in and took it. "Hello, Quinn."

Quinn might not be upset by Linda's attitude, but Chloe had to resist the urge to boot her mother right back out the door. "Tell him to call you Linda, Mother."

Her mother sent her a barbed look—then caught herself and said in a tight voice, "Yes. Please call me Linda."

"Will do."

Chloe gestured toward the sitting area, and they filed over there. Chloe and Quinn took the couch. Linda perched on one of the chairs.

"I thought maybe you would bring Dad with you," Chloe said.

Linda carefully placed her folded hands on her pressed-together knees. "He wanted to come. But I was under the impression it would be just the two of us, just... between us." She sent a disapproving glance in Quinn's direction and then swung her reproachful gaze right back to Chloe. "So I insisted that I would come alone." She cleared her throat, an officious little sound. "That's a beautiful ring. I hope...you'll be very happy." The words seemed to stick in her throat. Still, they were a definite improvement over the awful things she'd said about Quinn a few weeks ago and yesterday on the phone.

"Thank you, Linda," said Quinn.

Chloe put in, "Give Dad my love, will you?"

A grudging nod. And apparently, Linda had decided she'd had quite enough of making polite noises. "Now, what's this about?"

"It's about Ted, Mother."

Linda stiffened. "What more can possibly be said about Ted?"

"Well, Mom. In the past month, Ted has sent me flowers and then contacted me by email. I want nothing to do with him and I have told him that repeatedly. I've told *you* that often. But I got the impression from what you said at the first of the month that you and Ted have been in touch."

Her mother sniffed. "Oh. I see. Now it's my fault if Ted sent you flowers."

Quinn shifted beside Chloe. She reached over and touched his arm, reminding him of the agreement they'd made half an hour before—that he was there for support.

She said, "I'm going to ask you a direct question, Mom. I want a simple yes-or-no answer."

Linda wore her I-am-gravely-wounded face. "What is this, an interrogation?"

"Have you been in contact with Ted since I moved back to town? Yes or no?"

"I don't see what—"

Quinn spoke up then, his voice coaxing and gentle, "We just want your help, Linda. I realize that you know already, but I think it can't hurt to say again that Ted Davies wasn't a good husband to Chloe. He punched her more than once and he betrayed her with another woman."

"Well, I... Ahem. Yes, I'm aware. Chloe has told me all that."

Chloe took the lead again. She tried really hard to keep the antagonism out of her voice. "So, have you been in touch with him since I moved back to Justice Creek?"

"I don't..." Linda patted her hair, straightened her shoulders. And then, finally, she confessed, "He called me."

"How many times?"

"Once."

"When was that?"

"The middle of July. A week before we left for Maui. He was, well, you know how kind and flattering he's always been toward me. He just said he was thinking of me and hoping I was all right. At first, when he started talking, I reminded myself I needed to tell him that I didn't approve of the way he had treated you and I was going to say goodbye now and I didn't want him to contact me again. But then he just kept on talking and telling me how horrible he felt about how it had gone with the two of you. He said you were the best thing that had ever happened to him and he missed you every hour of every day. He said that things weren't going well with him and that new wife of his, that he deeply regretted letting you go. He just…seemed so sincere." She let out a small sound of honest distress and brought both her hands up. Pressing her fingers to her mouth, she looked at Chloe through pleading eyes.

Chloe made herself speak gently. "Ted is very good at seeming sincere."

Linda drew in a steadying breath and put her hands in her lap again. "Yes. Yes, he is. Before he hung up, he asked me not to tell you that he had called. He said that he…didn't want to cause any trouble."

Not cause any trouble? Ted? Now, that was a good one. "What did you tell him about me, Mother?"

"Nothing. I promise you. He did all the talking. At the end, he said he would like to send you a little card or something, just to say he was thinking of you. He asked for your address. But I told him I wasn't at liberty to give him any of your personal information. And he said of course, that was all right. He completely understood. He said if he decided to reach out to you, he would get your address some other way. He said it wouldn't be a problem. He seemed…very confident about that."

"I'll bet."

Linda's face crumpled, all her earlier bravado cracking to nothing, falling away. She cried, "All right. I just have to say this. I just have to tell you that I *have* been thinking, I truly have, since that horrible evening four weeks ago when you and I fought so bitterly about this. I need you to know that I… Chloe, oh, Chloe… I *know* I was wrong. I was wrong to listen to him at all, wrong not to tell him immediately to leave us alone and then hang up the phone, wrong not to tell you right away that he'd called me. He…well, he charmed me. He fed my ego. And I fell for his lies. But I did *not* tell him anything about you. I gave him no information. I swear it. I didn't!"

Quinn reached over and brushed the back of Chloe's hand. She glanced at him. His eyes spoke of forgiveness.

But Chloe wasn't to the point of forgiving her mother—not yet anyway. She said, "All right, Mom. I believe you. And the truth is if he's determined to reach me, I'm not that hard to find."

"That's what I *told* you, remember, four weeks ago, right before you…threw me out?"

"I remember. Did Ted say anything else?"

"Not that I can think of. Really, that was it. That was all. I haven't heard a word from him before or since."

"Did you tell Dad about that call?"

Linda shook her head. "Not until last night."

A little wave of relief washed through Chloe that her dad hadn't known, hadn't kept that secret from her, too.

Her mother went on. "After you called to say you wanted to speak with me tonight, I just got so upset about everything. I stewed over what you would say to me, knowing that I really did need to admit to you that Ted had called me, to tell you what he said. I just…well, I started crying and I couldn't stop. Your father was so worried. He had no idea what was the matter with me. I realized I couldn't keep the truth from him a minute longer. So I ended up telling him everything, beginning with the call from Ted and ending with exactly what happened when you and I fought four weeks ago."

"So he knows the whole story now?"

Her mother bobbed her head and fingered her pearls. "Your father's not very happy with me at the moment. I know I can't blame him for that. I only want you to know, Chloe, that I have been thinking about what I've done.

Not only thinking about how I've kept a secret of the fact that Ted called me. More than that. So much more. I've been thinking of the past, too."

"Mother, I—"

But Linda wouldn't quit. "No. Please. Don't stop me. I need to say this. I need you to know that I see now, I do. So many ways that I have been wrong. I've been thinking how very proud I was at your beautiful wine-country wedding. How sure I was that you had everything then— and that *I* deserved a lot of credit for how well you'd done, how I had worked so hard to make you the kind of woman you are, an accomplished woman who marries just the right man. I've done a lot of bragging, about you and your 'great' life down in San Diego."

"Mother, I just don't…" Her objections trailed off as Quinn's big hand covered hers. She drew strength from that simple touch, strength enough to let her mother continue. "Never mind. Go on."

"Thank you," Linda said. "Because there are so many ways I know that I've failed you. That first time you left Ted, when you came home to us and said you weren't happy with him? You said you were finished with him, you never wanted to go back. And what did I do? I pushed you to try again, to work it out, even though you told me he'd hit you, even though you said that sometimes he frightened you. I was so very proud of the fine life I thought you had, the life I had insisted you make for yourself—so proud, that I refused to see your desperate unhappiness. If I had listened to what you were telling me then, you might never have gone back to him. He wouldn't have hit you again. But you did go back. And he did hit you. And he betrayed you, too. And I see that I have to face all that now. I have to admit that it happened, to own my part in it. I have not been the mother that you deserve. But I want you to know, at least, that I do finally see how wrong I've been. I hope that someday you will find it in yourself to forgive me. I love you so much, Chloe Janine. You're the bright, shining star of my heart. I hate having to count all the ways I've let you down, all the—"

Chloe couldn't take any more. "Please stop."

Her mother shut her mouth and stared at her, stricken.

Chloe stood. "I would like you to leave now. I need a little time, you know? To process all this."

Linda gazed up at her, eyes brimming, mouth trembling, looking suddenly every one of her fifty-nine years. "Yes. Of course." She got up. "I understand. I'll just..." She waved her hand, a weak little gesture, as though she couldn't recall what she'd started to say. And then she turned to go.

Chloe followed her and pulled open the door.

Linda said in a small voice, "Please believe me. I am so sorry. And I hope that someday you'll give me another chance."

Chloe only nodded. She knew that if she said another word, she would lose it.

Quinn was right there, at her side. He said, "Linda, do you need me to drive you home?"

A single tear tracked down her cheek. She refused to wipe it away and she kept her chin high. "Thank you, Quinn. But I'll manage."

And then she went out into the fading light. Chloe stood in the open door and watched her walk along the breezeway to her car. As soon as she disappeared around the far corner of the garage, Chloe shut the door.

So gently, Quinn took her by the shoulders and turned her to face him. She didn't want to look at him. He always saw too damn much. But he put a finger under her chin and made her meet his waiting eyes.

That did it. With a hard sob, she threw herself against him.

His big arms closed around her. "Hey, now. Hey..."

Chloe held on tight to him and surrendered to her tears. She didn't even know for certain why she was crying.

Maybe it was the shock of seeing her mother like that—so broken and sad. Or maybe it was relief that for the first time in her memory, her mother had actually admitted that she'd been wrong.

Chapter Thirteen

Two weeks passed. They were good weeks, overall.

Monday through Saturday, Chloe's days were filled with work. When she got home, she went to the log house and had dinner with Quinn and family. At night, Quinn came to her. And most mornings by the time she woke up, he was gone.

He didn't mention setting a wedding date again. But she knew it was on his mind. It was on *her* mind, too. She wanted to move forward with their lives together. But she couldn't, not yet. Not until...

She wasn't sure what. She just felt she was waiting. It was like that old saying about the other shoe dropping. She wasn't really sure what the first shoe had been, but it had already fallen. And now she was just waiting for the other one to drop.

On the first Monday in September, Jody called her at Your Way to tell her she'd just refused a second order from Ted. Chloe felt no surprise. None. In her mind, she pictured one of those classic Christian Louboutin black patent pumps, the dagger-heeled ones with the signature red-lacquered soles. She pictured that beautiful shoe dangling from an unknown hand.

Not dropped. Not yet.

But soon, yes. Very soon.

Jody said she would email her the proof that Bloom had refused an order from Ted at Chloe's request. "But aside from that, I just wanted to give you a heads-up," she said.

"You're the best," Chloe said. "Quinn has such amazing sisters."

"Call me. Remember. If I can do anything..."

"You know I will."

Chloe had her self-defense class that evening. Her trainer in his padded suit didn't stand a chance. She went absolutely postal on the guy, screaming and kicking, punching and gouging. The instructor had to shout at her to stop fighting and run. Later, he reminded the class that the point of the exercise was to incapacitate the attacker long enough to get away, not to keep pounding on him once he'd let you go.

She went home that evening and put another entry in her TD file. She didn't tell Quinn about Jody's call. He knew there was something bothering her, but she insisted it was nothing. And she wasn't nearly as upset as she'd been the night she found the email from Ted. Quinn let it go, but he was watchful and edgy the rest of the night.

Yes, she knew she should tell him. She'd *promised* to tell him if Ted tried to get in touch in any way. And she would tell him. She wasn't actually keeping anything from him, she reasoned—not for long, anyway. Ted would find another way to get the flowers to her. And it would be soon. And she would tell Quinn about

Jody's call and the latest bouquet then. Two birds with one stone, you might say.

As long as Jody didn't let it slip to Quinn about refusing Ted's order before Ted sent more flowers, Chloe figured it would work out all right—not that there was anything right about any of this.

And actually, Chloe dreaded telling Quinn more than she did the inevitable appearance of the next floral masterpiece. Every time she told him about some move Ted had made on her, he got harder to convince that this was her problem to solve.

She truly did fear that the time would come when she wouldn't be able to hold Quinn back. He would go after Ted, do physical damage to Ted. And then what? If Quinn ended up in jail because of her…

Well, she just didn't know how she would bear that.

So, for the time being, she was breaking her promise to him, lying about Ted by omission. The issue of Ted was a wedge between them, a wedge that created an emotional gap, a gap that widened incrementally as the days passed and the problem remained unresolved. Her love for Quinn got stronger and stronger as time went by. And she knew the bond Quinn felt with her was equally as powerful.

But sometimes love and a soul-deep connection just weren't enough, not when he needed to protect her and she wouldn't let him do that. Not when he wanted to marry her and she kept putting him off.

She didn't have to wait long for that second bouquet of flowers.

It arrived the next day, Tuesday.

Like the other arrangement two months before, the flowers were waiting on her doorstep. She found them at a little after eight in the evening, when she came home from dinner across the street. She hadn't expected to be that upset when they came—after all, she knew they would be coming. But the sight hit her hard nonetheless.

Her blood roaring in her ears and her knees gone to jelly, she sank to the front step next to the cobalt-blue vase filled with bloodred roses. The little card in the plastic holder had Tilly's logo on it. But she could have guessed that without the card. The vase wasn't anywhere near as nice as the one from Bloom that she'd smashed in the compactor. And roses were always beautiful. But the whole presentation just came off as ordinary.

"Ordinary," she heard herself mutter under her breath. "No offense to Tilly's, but you're slipping a little, aren't you, Ted?" And then she laughed.

It was a slightly manic-sounding laugh, not altogether a sane laugh. But somehow, it helped. The laugh made her pulse slow, soothed the roaring of her blood in her ears and strengthened the odd weakness in her knees. She was able to grab the blue vase and rise to her feet.

Inside, she put the vase on the counter and read the card. *You're not marrying that guy. You know you're not. My darling, we need to talk.*

Ted

"Look on the bright side," she said to Quinn when he arrived an hour later and saw the roses in their blue vase right there on the counter where she had left them.

"Bright side?" He looked at her as though she'd said something in a language he didn't understand.

"Ted signed his name. I called Tilly's and they've agreed not to send me any more flowers from him. So next time he'll have to pay to have them sent from Boulder."

Quinn took a long time reading the card. Finally, he

said flatly, "There is no bright side. We both know that. Something's got to be done about this guy."

This was not going well. She'd known that it wouldn't. She really, really wished she hadn't told him. But lies didn't work; keeping the truth from him was no way to carry on a relationship.

She made herself tell him the rest, "Also, you should know that Jody called me yesterday to tell me he tried to send flowers through her."

His eyes flashed dark fire. "And last night when I asked you what was wrong, you lied and said there was nothing."

"I…" There she went with the one-word responses again. She made herself give him a few whole sentences by way of explanation. "I knew he would go through Tilly's next and that I was going to have to tell you soon. I didn't see any reason we had to fight twice over this. So I decided to tell you about both the call from Jody and the flowers, when they came, together."

His expression was set as a slab of granite. "You lied."

She threw up both hands. "Fine. All right. I lied. And I'm sorry."

"Are we in this together?" he demanded.

"Of course. Where are you leading me with that question?"

"I'm leading to the fact that 'together' means when something happens, you tell me *now*. And by now I mean, if Jody calls you with information, you call me as soon as you get off the phone with her. You don't store up the bad news to deliver in batches."

She really hated that he was right. "Yes. I get that. I won't do that again."

"And who says we're fighting?"

She felt so…tired suddenly. Just tired to her bones. "Look at you. You're furious at me."

"No. Not with you, angel. Never with you." He held up the little white card in his big, rough, wonderful hand. "This. Him. I need to deal with him."

"No. No, you do not need to deal with Ted. And you will *not* deal with Ted."

He shook the card at her. "He knows about me, knows you're with me." His voice was the low, focused rumble of some powerful predator, crouched and gathering to strike.

"Quinn, come on. That we're engaged wouldn't be all that difficult to find out."

"Not the point, Chloe. This card says I'm in this now. This card says—"

"That card says nothing of the kind. You know it doesn't." She dared to approach him. He watched her come with a stillness so total it raised the goose bumps on her skin. The need to take action seemed to radiate right out of his pores. When she stood in front of him, she said, "Put down the card."

"Chloe." Wary. Vigilant. And so very unwilling.

"Put down the card and put your arms around me."

He didn't. Not for several seconds. But then, finally, with a low oath, he dropped the card to the counter and hauled her close.

She wrapped her arms around him, too, as tight as she could. His big heart pounded, hard and insistent, under her ear. She lifted her head and looked up into his eyes. "If you play his game, you weaken us. You know you do."

He scanned her face, as though seeking the right point of entry. "I got demands. I need you to agree to them."

"This doesn't sound good."

"Hear me out."

She sighed. "Of course."

"Tomorrow, we take what little we've got in that file of yours and we go to the police station. They're gonna tell us that no crime has been committed and there's nothing they can do."

She got that. "But they'll write it up and then if he does make trouble, there's at least a record that we complained."

Quinn nodded. "And I don't like to think of you alone here. You move in with me."

She stepped back from the shelter of his arms. "Not yet. Uh-uh. Look, I really don't think he's that dangerous."

"The guy's a whack job, Chloe. You don't know what he's gonna do next."

She took a slow, calming breath. "As I was saying, if he did try anything, I'm not having that happen in the house where Annabelle lives."

"Annabelle." Quinn said his daughter's name thoughtfully.

"You know I'm right, Quinn. We don't want her traumatized by any of this. We just need to go on as we are for a little longer. That note says 'We have to talk.' I get the feeling he means soon." She was actually starting to hope that it *would* be soon, whatever it was. She wanted that other shoe to finally drop. "I'll be extra careful, I promise. I've got Mace and I know how to use it. Plus, you should see me in self-defense class. I'm outta control, I'm so bloodthirsty."

He grabbed her close again. "Don't make jokes about it."

"Sorry. Not funny, I know. The stress is kind of getting to me."

* * *

Chloe had Tai open the showroom for her the next morning, and Quinn took her to the Justice Creek Town Hall. They talked to Riley Grimes, a patrol officer who had been two years behind them at Justice Creek High. Riley went through Chloe's TD file and said he'd write a brief report of their visit for possible future reference. He suggested that they might try for an order of protection, known in some states as a restraining order. But that would be iffy, as Chloe had reported no incidents of abuse during her marriage and the evidence she'd gathered so far didn't indicate she was in any immediate danger.

Quinn was all for calling his half brother James, the lawyer in the family, and seeing if James thought they had a chance of getting a protection order.

Chloe vetoed that for now. "You heard what Riley said. Ted hasn't come near me. He hasn't broken into my house or even shown up in Justice Creek to have that 'talk' he mentioned. He hasn't threatened me in any way."

"Every move he makes is a threat. He's stalking you, Chloe. Aren't you clear on that yet?"

They were standing on the town hall steps. Chloe reached out and took his big, hard arm. "Can we talk about this in private, please—tonight, when we're alone?"

"Sure." He muttered the word out of the side of his mouth. "Whatever you say."

He drove her back to her house to get her car. When she headed up the front walk rather than straight to the garage, he got out and followed her.

"What now?" She stopped to face him on the front step.

He had that look. Grim. Uncompromising. "I thought you were going to the showroom."

"I will. In a little while. I've got some samples I brought home last night I want to take back with me. And then I'm stopping at your house down the hill to touch base with Nell on the remodeling."

"Lock the door behind you when you go in, and reset the alarm while you're in there—on second thought, I'll just wait here until you're ready to get in your car."

"Quinn." She reached out and put her hand against his bleak-looking face. Tenderness flooded her. Oh, she did love him. And one of these days, she really needed to gather the courage to tell him so. "Please stop worrying and go to work. You can't watch over me every hour of every day."

His eyes had a strange gleam to them, bright and dark, both at once. "I don't like this."

She tried for humor. "I think you might have mentioned that once or twice already."

The corners of his mouth failed to twitch even the slightest bit. "I know more than one good man in personal security—"

"No. I mean it. Don't you even start talking bodyguards. You're overreacting. I do not need a bodyguard."

He hooked a big arm around her and hauled her up close against him. As always, she reveled in the heat, the sheer power of him. "You watch yourself. Promise me. Stay aware."

"I will."

He swooped down and kissed her hard and quick. "We're talking more about this tonight."

A resigned sigh escaped her. "Yes, I'm quite clear on that."

He kissed her once more, as swift and sweetly punishing as the time before, and then, finally, he let her go and returned to his car. She waited until he started up the engine and backed from the space beside the garage before letting herself in the house. After locking herself in and rearming the alarm, she ran downstairs to collect her samples and hurried right back up.

The blinking red light on the answering machine caught her attention as she was about to go out the door. She almost left it for later. But it could be something important.

Turned out it was a hang-up call. A swift ripple of unease slithered down her spine, followed by a burst of anger. *Thank you so much, Ted. Now even a hang-up call freaks me out.*

She considered trying *69. But what for? Whoever was on the other end, she didn't want to talk to them.

Enough. She made herself a promise to banish her jerk of an ex-husband from her mind for the rest of the day.

And she kept that promise.

Until she got home from dinner at Quinn's and found two more hang-up calls on her phone. When she went ahead and tried to call back, she learned that both calls were from blocked numbers. That thoroughly creeped her out. Though she had no proof of who had made the calls, she added them to her TD file and tried not to stew over them.

Then Quinn showed up.

Of course, he knew right away that something had happened. "What?" he said when he was barely in the door. "Just tell me."

So she told him about the hang up calls.

His expression grew even bleaker. "You put it in the file?"

"I did, yes. I noted the date and the times that the calls came in and that whoever made them did it from a blocked number. In case it somehow turns out to matter in some way."

"We need to talk about you trying for that order of protection."

She went over, dropped to the sofa and put her head in her hands. "Can we just…not? Please?" She looked up. He was standing over her, eyes stormy with equal parts anger and concern. She got up. "He's running our lives, Quinn. We can't let him do that."

He clasped her shoulders in his big hands and pressed his forehead to hers. "I've been thinking."

"Thinking about…?" She tipped her face back enough to look at him—and then she lifted enough to touch his lips with hers.

He made that low, lovely growling sound in his throat and settled his mouth more firmly on hers. They shared a slow, delicious kiss. He gathered her in. She slid her hands up over his chest and linked them behind his neck.

"Now, that's what I'm talking about," she said softly, when he finally lifted his head.

"Vegas." He bent and kissed the word onto her up-turned mouth. And then, soft as a breath, back and forth, he brushed his lips against hers and whispered, "This weekend. We'll fly to Vegas and get married."

"Married?" She jerked back so that their lips no longer touched. "Quinn, we've talked about that."

He scowled. "I know that tone of voice. Here come all the damn objections."

"I meant what I said before. I just need a little more time, that's all."

"Uh-uh. You need to be my wife and live with me and Annabelle and Manny. I don't want you living alone here. Not anymore."

"I'm perfectly safe. You're here half the time and a

lot of the time I'm at your house. And what about Anna-belle? I don't want to put her in danger, I really don't."

"So you do admit you're in danger."

Sometimes the man was too quick by half. "No, no, of course I'm not in danger."

"Listen to yourself, angel. You're 'perfectly safe,' but you're afraid that if you move in with us, you'll put my little girl in danger. You're all over the map about this."

"No, that's not so. I really don't think anything is going to happen. But if something did, I couldn't stand it if Annabelle ended up in the middle of it."

He took her by the shoulders—carefully, but firmly, too. "A few minutes ago, you said that we couldn't let that guy run our lives."

"And I meant it!"

"Then stop."

She searched his face, not following. "Stop...?"

"You're letting him keep you from living your life. You're putting everything on hold for him."

"No."

"Yeah, Chloe. Yeah, you are. How long you gonna do that to yourself, huh? How long you gonna do that to *us*?"

She stared up at him, her heart like a stone, so heavy in her chest. She knew he was right.

And yet she just couldn't do it. Not now. She could not say her love out loud. And she couldn't agree to get married. Not right now. Not until she'd somehow dealt with the problem that was Ted.

Quinn didn't know what to do about Chloe.

She tied his hands at every turn. She wouldn't let him make a move on her ex. She wouldn't marry him and live with him in his house where he could better protect her. She wouldn't let him hire someone to watch over her. She wouldn't let his half brother James check into slapping good old Ted with an order of protection.

She had dark circles under her ice-blue eyes and much of the time she seemed distant and distracted. He only had her full attention when he took her to bed.

Something had to give.

And it had damn well better give soon. She seemed so fragile to him lately and he feared some kind of… breakage. He feared the destruction of what they had together—no, worse. He feared the ruin of her tender heart, her strength, her spirit.

That night, he held her as she slept and wondered what the hell to do.

When Chloe woke in the morning, Quinn was still there. Already dressed in the jeans and knit shirt he'd worn the night before, he sat in the bedside chair, just looking at her.

She pushed up on an elbow and raked her sleep-tangled hair back off her forehead. "Shouldn't you be having breakfast with Annabelle?"

He rose. "I'm going now. I was just waiting for you to wake up."

She saw the shadows in his eyes and felt remorse drag at her—for giving him nothing but trouble lately, for being a source of constant concern. "I'm perfectly safe here. All the locks are sturdy and the alarm system is state-of-the-art. And I promise to keep the system armed when you're not here and to stay alert whenever I'm outside on my own."

He bent close, brushed a kiss on her forehead and said mildly, "I just wanted to wait until you were awake."

She started to accuse him of lying. He'd stayed to watch over her and they both knew that.

But she came to her senses before she could light into

him. He only wanted to take care of her. Had she sunk to snapping at him for trying to keep her safe?

She ended up asking sheepishly, "Give Annabelle a kiss for me?"

He promised that he would and then he was gone.

Wearily, she got up and went about the beginnings of another day.

At a little after eight, as she was eating breakfast, the phone rang. She let out a cry at the sound and splashed hot coffee across the back of her hand. Wanting to slap her own face for being such a nervous twit, she mopped up the spill with a paper napkin and picked up the phone.

It was only Tai calling in sick. "It's just a cold," she said. "I'm thinking if I take it easy today, I'll be ready to go again by tomorrow." Chloe told her to get plenty of rest and drink lots of liquids, and Tai laughed and said, "Yes, Dr. Winchester. I'll take good care of myself."

Chloe left the house at eight-thirty, arming the alarm and locking things up tight. She kept her eyes open and her head up as she crossed the breezeway to the garage. She was careful in the garage, standing in the open doorway to the breezeway, pushing the button on the wall that sent the main door rattling up and then having a quick look around the space before shutting and relocking the breezeway door behind her. Locking herself in the car, she backed from the garage and then sat there until the door was all the way down, just to be certain Ted didn't dart in there when she wasn't looking, to lie in wait for her later.

At Your Way, she exercised the same watchfulness, scanning the little lot behind the building for any lurkers before she got out of the car. And then getting out quickly, locking the doors and hustling toward the back entrance, her right hand in a fist and her keys poking out between her fingers, a makeshift weapon ready to gouge a few nasty holes in anybody foolish enough to jump her.

She didn't fiddle or linger, but quickly unlocked the back door, disarmed the alarm and locked the door behind her. Then she went through the rooms—the office, the restroom, the studio in back and the showroom in front.

Ted was not waiting there. Everything was right where she'd left it the evening before.

And did she feel foolish and overcautious and strangely let down?

Yes, a little bit. But she'd kept her word to Quinn, kept her head up and all her senses on alert, just as they'd taught her in self-defense class, all the way from her front door to the showroom.

Truthfully being vigilant was nerve-racking. And her nerves lately had been racked quite enough, thank you.

She spruced up the showroom and got the coffee going. At nine, she unlocked the front door and turned the sign around. Then she went behind the register counter and called Nell over at Bravo Construction to say she was stuck at the store until closing time but would stop by the remodeling site on the way home.

Nell was her usual bold, funny self. One of the new guys on the crew had asked her to dinner. "Big muscles," Nell said, "gorgeous ink. Too bad the brain is practically nonexistent. I like a big brain. It matters to me."

"So he's only a piece of tasty meat and you're not going out with him?"

"Tasty meat." Nell groaned. "I said that, didn't I, when I was busting your chops about Quinn?"

"You most definitely did."

Call-ump. Call-ump. Chloe recognized the sound of

Nell's boots landing on her scarred desktop. Nell said, "So you think I'm objectifying this guy?"

"Well, maybe just a little."

"You know, he *is* really sweet. Is it his fault he's no Einstein? Dumb guys need love, too. And he's so pretty to look at."

Chloe thought of Quinn, who was not only wonderful to look at with a heart of pure gold, he was brilliant, as well. She felt an ache down inside her, just thinking of him. Because she loved him so, because she kept pushing him away when she knew she ought to be grabbing him closer, holding on tight, promising never, ever, to let him go.

She reminded Nell, "People used to think Quinn was slow, remember? And you *can* be pretty intimidating."

"Me? You're kidding."

"You're a force to be reckoned with, Nellie."

"Keep talkin'. I'm startin' to like where this is going."

"Did you ever stop to think that maybe the guy is shy?"

"Oh, and I freak him out because I'm so awesome?"

"Nell, you are a giant bowl of awesome—with extra whipped cream and cherries on top. So yeah, it's more than possible he's intimidated by you."

"A giant bowl of awesome. I like the sound of that a lot. And so you're saying I should give this guy a chance?"

"Yeah. I think you should. He might turn out to be smarter than you think."

Nell said she'd give it more thought. And then, out of nowhere, she asked, "Baby, are you okay?"

Chloe's throat instantly clutched and tears burned behind her eyes. "Ahem." She turned around and faced the hallway to the back door. Swiping at her eyes, she spoke more softly. "Fine. I'm fine."

"Stop lyin' to me, Chloe. It's so not working."

Chloe gulped down a fresh spurt of tears. "Really, I don't even know where to start…"

"Is it Quinn? If he's causing you grief—"

Chloe let out a laugh that caught on a sob. "Wait a minute. Aren't you the one who asked me if I was slumming with your brother and promised to hurt me if I wasn't good to him?"

"That was before I knew you. I was wrong, all wrong. You and Quinn are a great match, a true love match. And I love you both."

Chloe's throat clutched all over again. "Oh, Nellie. Thank you."

"No need for thanks. We're family."

"And that makes me so glad."

"But the problem is…?"

"Well, I can say this much. Quinn is *not* the problem. He's the best thing that ever happened to me and I love him so much and somehow I don't know how to tell him so. Things are scary right now and—"

"Scary, how?"

"Long story. I'll only say that sometimes I think I'm just too damaged, you know? I think that there's really something very wrong with me and I'm afraid that's never going to change."

"Not a damn thing is wrong with you. And we need some sister time."

Chloe started to object. But then she realized she *did* want some sister time with Nell. "You know, that sounds really good."

"Instead of the remodel, let's meet at McKellan's. Best cosmos in Colorado." The entry chime sounded. Chloe swiped at her cheeks again and tried to compose herself before turning to greet her first customer of the day.

Nell said, "Five-fifteen. Be there. Call Quinn and tell him that there will be drinking and he might have to pick us up later."

"I will. See you. McKellan's. Five-fifteen." Chloe sniffed and smoothed her hair. Then she turned around and carefully set the receiver in its cradle.

When she finally glanced up with a bright smile for whoever had come in, Ted was standing not twenty feet away in front of the showroom door.

Chapter Fourteen

Chloe's heart beat a sick rhythm under her ribs and her throat felt like some invisible hand was squeezing it tight.

She'd done it to herself. It was all her own fault. She'd let down her guard. She'd turned around and forgotten all about how she needed to keep her head up and her eyes front.

She'd let her concentration slip to cry on Nellie's shoulder—and her nightmare had found her.

Somehow he'd not only slipped in the door when she was talking to Nell, but he'd whipped the open sign around, too. It was just a regular glass door with a knob lock you could turn from the inside.

She had zero doubt he'd locked it, as well.

Her nightmare had not only found her, he'd locked himself in her showroom with her.

Beautifully turned out as always in a perfectly tailored designer suit and a Seven Fold Robert Talbott tie, not a single dark blond hair out of place, he gave her a slow, charming smile. And then he said in that smooth, cool voice that had slowly turned all her dreams into nightmares, "Hello, Chloe."

Her purse was under the counter. She needed to reach in there and pull out the Mace. Carefully, trying not to move the upper part of her body and give herself away, she felt for the purse, found it...

Oh, God, she'd zipped it shut. He would know if she tried to get it open now.

Run! She needed to get the hell out of there. She started to whirl for the back door.

Ted said, so very mildly, "Please don't do that."

And her mind went to mush as her legs started shaking. She was rooted to the spot.

It was pitiful, really. Such a sad case, she was. He had trained her so well over all those awful, endless years with him. He only had to look at her, only had to speak to her in that smooth, mild voice of his and she couldn't fall all over herself fast enough to do whatever he demanded of her.

She had dared, in the past year, to believe herself free of him—well, except for the nightmares. She had *made* herself free of him. She'd divorced him and moved on, found Quinn. *Her* Quinn, so fine and true, everything she'd always wanted—only better. Only *more...*

She shut her eyes. No. She couldn't think of Quinn now. She needed to focus, needed to remember her self-defense training, to start acting like the independent, self-possessed, self-directed woman she actually was.

And yet, somehow, she stood there, just *stood* there, and did nothing as Ted came for her.

With his fine Italian shoes light and quick on the showroom's wood floor, he walked right up to the counter, stepped around it, and wrapped his perfectly manicured hand around her upper arm. "You're beautiful, my darling, as always. But you look tired."

The faint smell of the signature cologne he always had specially made just for him came to her. She knew she would gag on that smell. But she swallowed, hard, and glanced down at his fingers encircling her arm. "Where's your wedding ring, Ted?"

He actually chuckled. "Larissa and I are through."

"I'm so sorry to hear that."

"No, you're not. You knew all along she wouldn't last. A diversion, that's all she was supposed to be. I work very hard, and you know that I do, to make a fine life for us. I deserve a diversion now and then. But then you left me and I tried to distract myself, tried to convince myself that any beautiful, reasonably intelligent woman would do. I thought I could forget you. I was wrong. You are mine, and you are perfect for me and I'm ready now to give you another chance."

She simply could not let that pass. "But I'm not yours."

"Yes, you are."

"We're divorced, Ted, in case you've forgotten. And the last thing I want is another chance with you."

His eyes shifted, away—and then back. Other than that, he pretended he hadn't heard her. "Let's sit down, shall we?"

"I don't want to sit down with you. Let go of my arm, Ted. Leave. Now. Please."

Again, he ignored her. "This way." He started walking, pulling her with him, into the hallway that led to the back door, pausing at the open arch on the left. "This will do." He led her into her studio and over to her worktable, where he pulled out a chair and pushed her down in it. Then he grabbed another chair a few feet away and yanked it over next her. He sat down, too. And then he said, "I love you, my darling. And I've come to take you home. I know that I hurt you and I swear to you that I will never do that again." He reached out. She steeled herself not to cringe away as he traced the line of her hair along her cheek and down her neck.

Chloe's skin crawled. She swallowed bile again and stared at her worktable, taking a strange kind of comfort from the tools she used every day: the stacks of thick fabric sample books, the color wheels, the sketch tablets, the loose swatches of fabric, the scissors, drafting compass, tape measure, shape templates, colored pencils and fine-point pens...

Ted kept on talking. "I called you three times yesterday. You never picked up. And then I thought, well, that's all right. It's better that we talk face-to-face anyway. Better that we cut to the chase and you can just come home with me. And it *is* better. It's wonderful to see you, my darling. And now I just want you to look at me. I want you to tell me the truth, that you've missed me and you're so glad to see me. I want to work this out with you—and yes, I know. My temper has been a problem. But I'll return to counseling. Everyone needs a little extra help getting things right now and then."

She tried again. "Ted. I'm in love with my fiancé and I don't want anything to do with you."

"You don't mean that."

"Yes, Ted, I do."

"Look at me." He grabbed her chin in a punishing grip and yanked her head around to face him.

"That's going to leave a bruise." She glared at him.

"Darling, I'm so sorry."

"I don't believe you." She realized she was getting

less numb and more angry. Angry was good. At least her knees weren't shaking anymore.

"You know, Chloe. You really shouldn't bait me. If you would only treat me with the love and respect I deserve, our lives would go so smoothly, everything just so, moving along without a hitch."

She shot to her feet.

But before she could dodge around him and make for the door, he grabbed her hand. "Sit *down*." And he yanked her back into the chair so hard that her teeth clacked together. "What's this?" He still had her hand. Her left hand.

"It's my engagement ring. Remember? I'm engaged." She tried to pull away.

He held on. His face was getting that look, his eyes distant, his skin flushing mottled red. "Take it off."

"You'll have to let go for me to do that."

But he didn't let go. "Already, you are out of hand. You are pushing me too far. You know that you are."

"Let go of me, Ted."

"Don't you ever try to tell me what to do."

"Let me go," she said softly. And then she said it again, a little louder, "Let me go." And then she couldn't *stop* saying it, louder and louder, "Let me go, let me go, let me go, let me go…"

And right then, as she repeated that same phrase like a mantra, for the seventh time, he drew back his fist and he punched her in the jaw.

Chloe saw stars as blood filled her mouth. It hurt—and more than just the fist to the face. She'd bitten her own tongue, bitten it good and hard.

Everything got very clear then. Crystal clear.

She needed to defend herself and she needed to do it now.

Chloe let out a scream. It was a wild cry, feral. Furious. Ted stared at her, bug-eyed in surprise. His perfect darling Chloe would never let out such an animal sound—a tasteful little whimper, maybe. But a full-out, full-throated scream of rage? No way.

However, she was no longer his perfect Chloe. She belonged to herself now—to herself, and to Quinn. She needed to end all of Ted's false assumptions and she needed to end them forever and always.

So she reached over, grabbed one of the heavy sample books in both hands, drew it back and whacked that sucker right across the side of his big, fat head. His chair scraped the floor as the sample book connected. He let out a grunt of surprise.

And that was all he got a chance to do.

Because she went kind of crazy. She lifted that sample book and she hit him again. His chair went over and he was on the floor. She jumped on top of him and hit him some more.

By then he was making these ridiculous little whining sounds, his arms drawn up in front of his face. He was calling her name, "Chloe, stop! Chloe, don't!" as she flailed at him with the sample book.

From out in the showroom came pounding and shouts, followed by the sound of glass shattering. And then, wonder of wonders, Quinn's voice: "Chloe!"

"Back here!" She climbed off Ted and stood, panting, above him, still holding the sample book threateningly over her head, as Quinn came flying into the room.

"Angel, my God…"

About then, she noticed there was blood all down the front of her white silk shirt. She explained mildly, her tongue already swelling in her mouth, "He hit me and I bit my tongue."

On the floor, Ted was curled in the fetal position. "Help me," he groaned. "Get that crazy bitch away from me!"

Quinn said, "This must be Ted." Chloe dropped the sample book on the table, pressed her suddenly quivering lips together and nodded. He asked, "How bad are you hurt?"

"I'm okay, really. It lookth worth than it ith."

Ted rolled and started to get up.

Quinn said flatly, "Stay on the floor, Ted."

With a moan, Ted went over on his side and curled up in a ball. He whined, "You people are insane."

"Just shut up and don't move."

Surprisingly, Ted took Quinn's advice.

Chloe zipped past Ted and got to Quinn. He hooked his big arm around her, pressed his warm lips to her forehead and whispered, "I think he's got your message now. You did good, angel. Real good."

She snuggled in close to him. "How did you know to come here?"

"Nell called me. Told me you'd been cryin' on the phone and I'd better get the hell over here and not leave until all your doubts were dealt with and all your tears were dried."

"I love Nell."

"Yeah, well, for once I guess I won't be pissed at her for sticking her nose in." He kissed her forehead again. "You're okay, you're sure?"

"I am. I really am."

"Good, then. Go call 911. Use the phone in the showroom."

It occurred to Chloe that it might not be such a great idea to leave Ted alone with Quinn. "Pleathe don't hit Ted," she whispered. "He'th not worth it."

"I'm not going to hit him. I'm only going to do what I've always wanted to do and that is to have a little talk with him."

"Quinn, I really don't think—"

"Angel."

"What?"

"Go on. Make that call."

What Quinn said to Ted, only Ted ever knew.

Whatever it was, when Chloe reentered the back studio room after calling the police station, Ted was sitting in the chair again. He had nicks and scratches all over his face, and his right eye was swiftly turning a deep magenta. His tie was askew, his fine suit wrinkled and his hair a mess. He told her quietly that he'd been way out of line and he was very sorry and he would not be bothering her anymore.

She believed him. Now that he knew she would fight him, he wouldn't get near her again. She really was tempted to leave it at that. Pressing charges could be messy. He'd probably string the process out forever. Who knew what tricks he might try?

But she kind of wondered if he'd ever hit Larissa. And if, for the third time, she just let it go, would he only find another woman to bully and hurt?

So when Riley Grimes showed up, she told him and his partner exactly what had happened. By then, she had a doozey of a bruise swelling at her jaw. The blood down the front of her made its own statement about what Ted had done to her. Her tongue thick and slow and very painful, she told them exactly what had happened and said that yes, she did intend to press charges. So Riley and the other officer took Ted away in handcuffs. They'd called an ambulance for her. Quinn had smashed the glass in the front door, so he got hold of his brother Carter to come over and secure the showroom entrance. Then he went with Chloe in the ambulance to the hospital southeast of town.

At Justice Creek General, they took pictures of her injuries and an X-ray of her jaw. Nothing was broken. Her tongue was a mess. They advised saltwater rinses, ice packs and aloe vera gel. The good news? The bleeding had stopped on its own. The doctor said that if she still had pain in a week, she should see her family practitioner.

Quinn hovered close, and Chloe loved that he did. She knew she was going to be fine now. Yes, her face ached, her tongue throbbed and she was talking with a lisp. But all of that was temporary. Down inside, in her heart and soul, she'd never felt better.

She'd never felt so free.

Quinn couldn't wait to get her home to Annabelle and Manny, though he did kind of worry that she might give him grief about it, might demand that he take her to her house.

But no. She just smiled with that beautiful, battered face of hers and said, "Yeth. Take me home to Annabelle and Manny. Thath where I want to be."

At home, Quinn told Manny what had happened. Manny settled Chloe on the sofa with a mountain of pillows at her back and a light blanket over her knees. He brought her an ice pack and a saltwater rinse for her poor, aching tongue.

When Annabelle came bouncing down the stairs, they told her that Chloe had been hurt and she needed them to take care of her. Annabelle demanded to be allowed to kiss the boo-boo on Chloe's jaw and make it all better. She insisted that Chloe have her one-eyed teddy bear. "Hug him real hard, Chloe. Then you will feel much better."

Quinn called Nell to let her know what had gone down. Nell turned right around and called everybody. Within half an hour, family members started arriving. By late afternoon, Chloe had had visits from all of Quinn's sisters and three of his brothers.

Nell even called Chloe's parents. Linda and Doug Winchester rushed right over. Chloe took it well, Quinn thought. She let her dad hug her and then her mom, too. Linda cried. She pulled Quinn aside and said she needed to tell him personally how very wrong she'd been. She hoped, she said, that someday, somehow, she would find a way to make things right with her daughter and with him.

He gave her a hug and told her there was nothing to make right. "We're family now, Linda. Everything's going to be just fine."

That caused Linda to cry even harder.

Then Doug clapped him on the back. "I know I don't have to say it. But I'm a father and that means I'll say it anyway. Take good care of my little girl. She hasn't had it easy."

"I will, sir," Quinn promised. "You can count on me."

Then Doug took Linda home.

Chloe made a list of what she needed from her house. Quinn went over there and gathered everything up.

And that night, for the first time, he had her in his bed where he'd always wanted her. He brought her aspirin for the pain and he wrapped himself around her and he held her all night long.

Chloe never went back to the house across the street. Slowly, she and Quinn and Manny moved everything she needed to the log house.

Within a week, her tongue was fully functional again. On a Thursday night late, she and Quinn sat out under the stars and said the things they'd never managed to say before.

She told him what was in her heart. "I love you, Quinn. So, so much."

And he said, "I love you, angel. I've been wanting to tell you forever. But somehow the time never seemed right."

"I think maybe you sensed that I wasn't ready yet. To say it. To hear it. But I'm ready *now*."

"Yeah," he said gruffly. "I see that. I feel that. I love you, Chloe Winchester." He stared deep in her eyes.

She gazed back at him and knew she'd gotten it exactly right the second time around. "I went all wrong there, for so many years."

"No."

"Yes. I went wrong, took the wrong path. But I'm back where I belong now. I think deep down I always knew you were the one for me, from way back when we were little, from when you used to put those Hershey's Kisses on Miss Oakleaf's desk."

He groaned. "You remember that? Nobody remembers that."

"Well, yeah. We all kind of do." She got up from her deck chair—but only so that she could sit on his lap. Wrapping her arms around his neck, she whispered in his ear, "It was so sweet and so romantic, you leaving chocolate for Miss Oakleaf. Everybody said so."

"You think so, huh?"

"I do, yes."

"I love you, Chloe." He nuzzled her hair. "I love you. Now that I'm finally saying it, I just can't say it enough."

"Good. Because I love you, too."

"Vegas?" he asked, his mouth so warm and soft against her cheek.

She turned her head—just enough so that their lips could meet. They shared a long, sweet kiss. And then she answered him, "Vegas. Definitely. Name the day."

Five weeks later, they moved back to the fully renovated house down the hill. Annabelle put on her fairy princess costume and danced around her new princess bedroom, scattering fairy dust as she went. That same day, Manny presented her with a tiny, long-haired, big-eared Chihuahua puppy, which she promptly named Mouse.

And a week after that, Quinn and Chloe were married in the wedding chapel at High Sierra Resort and Casino in Las Vegas on the Sunset Strip. Annabelle was the flower girl. Manny stood up as best man. Quinn's sisters and Tracy Winham and Rory Bravo-Calabretti were all bridesmaids, with Nell the maid of honor.

Doug Winchester proudly gave his only daughter away for the second time. "This is the one that counts," he whispered to Chloe as he walked her down the aisle to Quinn. Linda Winchester cried all through the ceremony—tears of joy, she said.

For Chloe, it was the happiest day of her life.

So far.

* * * * *

*Don't miss CARTER BRAVO'S CHRISTMAS BRIDE,
the next installment in Christine Rimmer's
THE BRAVOS OF JUSTICE CREEK miniseries,
coming in December 2015,
only from Harlequin Special Edition.*

DEVIN CONCENTRATED, NIBBLING on her bottom lip as she tried to work the needles that seemed unwieldy and awkward, no matter how she tried.

After her third time tangling the yarn into a total mess, Devin sighed and admitted defeat. Again. Every time they happened to be assigned to work together, Greta took a moment to try teaching her to knit. And every time, she came up short.

"People who find knitting at all relaxing have to be crazy. I think I must have some kind of mental block. It's just not coming."

"You're not trying hard enough," Greta insisted.

"I am! I swear I am."

"Even my eight-year-old granddaughter can do it," she said sternly. "Once you get past the initial learning curve, this is something you'll love the rest of your life."

"I think it's funny." Callie Bennett, one of the other

nurses and also one of Devin's good friends, smirked as she observed her pitiful attempts over the top of her magazine.

"Oh, yes. Hilarious," Devin said drily.

"It is! You're a physician who can set a fractured radius, suture a screaming six-year-old's finger and deliver a baby, all with your eyes closed."

"Not quite," Devin assured her. "I open my eyes at the end of childbirth so I can see to cut the umbilical cord."

Callie chuckled. "Seriously, you're one of the best doctors at this hospital. I love working with you and wish you worked here permanently. You're cool under pressure and always seem to know just how to deal with every situation. But I hate to break it to you, hon, you're all thumbs when it comes to knitting, no matter how hard you try."

"I'm going to get the hang of this tonight," she insisted. "If Greta's eight-year-old granddaughter can do it, so can I."

She picked up the needles again and concentrated under the watchful eye of the charge nurse until she'd successfully finished the first row of what she hoped would eventually be a scarf.

"Not bad," Greta said. "Now, just do that about four hundred more times and you might have enough for a decent-sized scarf."

Devin groaned. Already, she was wishing she had stuck to reading the latest medical journals to pass the time instead of trying to knit yet again.

"I've got to go back to my office and finish the schedule for next month," Greta said. "Keep going and remember—ten rows a day keeps the psychiatrist away."

Devin laughed but didn't look up from the stitches.

"How do you always pick the slowest nights to fill in?" Callie asked after Greta left the nurses' station.

"I have no idea. Just lucky, I guess."

It wasn't exactly true. Her nights weren't always quiet. The past few times she had substituted for the regular emergency department doctors at Lake Haven Hospital had been low-key like this one, but that definitely wasn't always the case. A month earlier, she worked the night of the first snowfall and had been on her feet all night, between car accidents, snow shovel injuries and a couple of teenagers who had taken a snowmobile through a barbed-wire fence.

Like so much of medicine, emergency medicine was all a roll of the dice.

Devin loved her regular practice as a family physician in partnership with Russell Warrick, who had been her own doctor when she was a kid. She loved having a day-to-day relationship with her patients and the idea that she could treat an entire family from cradle to grave.

Even so, she didn't mind filling in at the emergency department when the three rotating emergency medicine physicians in the small hospital needed an extra hand. The challenge and variety of it exercised her brain and sharpened her reflexes—except tonight, when the only thing sharp seemed to be these knitting needles that had become her nemesis.

She was on her twelfth row when she heard a commotion out in the reception area.

"We need a doctor here, right now."

"Can you tell me what's going on?" Devin heard the receptionist ask in a calm voice.

Devin didn't wait around to hear the answer. She and Callie both sprang into action. Though the emergency department usually followed triage protocol, with prospective patients screened by one of the certified nurse assistants first to determine level of urgency, that seemed superfluous when the newcomers were the only patients here. By default, they automatically moved to the front of the line, since there wasn't one.

She walked through the doorway to the reception desk and her initial impression was of a big, tough-looking man, a very pregnant woman in one of the hospital wheelchairs and a couple of scared-looking kids.

"What's the problem?"

"Are you a doctor?" the man demanded. "I know how emergency rooms work. You tell your story to a hundred different people before you finally see somebody who can actually help you. I don't want to go through that."

She gave a well-practiced smile. "I'm Dr. Shaw, the attending physician here tonight. What seems to be the problem?"

"Devin? Is that you?"

The pregnant woman looked up and met her gaze and Devin immediately recognized her. "Tricia! Hello."

Tricia Barrett had been a friend in high school, though she hadn't seen her in years. Barrett had been her maiden name, anyway. Devin couldn't remember the last name of the man she married.

"Hi," Tricia said, her features pale and her arms tight on the armrests of the wheelchair. "I would say it's great to see you again, but, well, not really, under these circumstances. No offense."

Devin stepped closer to her and gave her a calming smile. "None taken. Believe me, I get it. Why don't you tell me what's going on."

Tricia shifted in the wheelchair. "Nothing. Someone is overreacting."

"She slipped on a patch of ice about an hour ago and hurt her ankle." The man with her overrode her objections. "I'm not sure it's broken but she needs an X-ray."

At first she thought he might be Tricia's husband but on closer inspection, she recognized him, only because she'd seen him around town here and there over the past few years.

Cole Barrett, Tricia's older brother, was a rather hard man to overlook—six feet two inches of gorgeousness, with vivid blue eyes, sinfully long eyelashes and sun-streaked brown hair usually hidden by a cowboy hat.

He had been wild back in the day, if she remembered correctly, and still hadn't lost that edgy, bad-boy out-law vibe.

In a small community like Haven Point, most people knew each other—or at least knew *of* each other. She hadn't met the man but she knew he lived in the mountains above town and that he had inherited a sprawling, successful ranch from his grandparents.

If memory served, he had once been some kind of hotshot rodeo cowboy.

With that afternoon shadow and his wavy brown hair a little disordered, he looked as if he had just climbed either off a horse or out of some lucky woman's bed. Not that it was any of her business. Disreputable cowboys were definitely *not* her type.

Devin dismissed the man from her mind and focused instead on her patient, where her attention should have been in the first place.

"Have you been able to put weight on your ankle?"

"No, but I haven't really tried. This is all so silly," Tricia insisted. "I'm sure it's not broken."

She winced suddenly, her face losing another shade or two of color, and pressed a hand to her abdomen.

Devin didn't miss the gesture and her attention sharpened. "How long have you been having contractions?"

"I'm sure they're only Braxton Hicks."

"How far along are you?"

"Thirty-four weeks. With twins, if you couldn't tell by the basketball here."

Her brother frowned. "You're having contractions? Why didn't you say anything?"

"Because you're already freaking out over a stupid sprained ankle. I didn't want to send you into total panic mode."

"What's happening?" the girl said. "What are contractions?"

"It's something a woman's body does when she's almost ready to have a baby," Tricia explained.

"Are you having the babies *tonight*?" she asked, big blue eyes wide. "I thought they weren't supposed to be here until after Christmas."

"I hope not," Tricia answered. "Sometimes I guess you have practice contractions. I'm sure that's what these are."

For the first time, she started to look uneasy and Devin knew she needed to take control of the situation.

"I don't want to send you up to obstetrics until we take a look at the ankle. We can hook up all the fetal monitoring equipment down here in the emergency department to see what's going on and put your minds at ease."

"Thanks. I'm sure everything's fine. I'm going to be embarrassed for worrying everyone."

"Never worry about that," Devin assured her.

"I'm sorry to bother you, but I need to get some information so we can enter it into the computer and make an ID band." Brittney Calloway, the receptionist, stepped forward, clipboard in hand.

"My insurance information is in my purse," Tricia said. "Cole, can you find it and give her what she needs."

He looked as if he didn't want to leave his sister's side but the little boy was already looking bored.

Whose were they? The girl looked to be about eight, blonde and ethereal like Tricia but with Cole's blue eyes, and the boy was a few years younger with darker coloring and big brown eyes.

She hadn't heard the man had kids—in fact, as far as she knew, he had lived alone at Evergreen Springs the past year since his grandmother died.

"You can come back to the examination room after you're done out here, or you can stay out in the waiting room."

He looked at the children and then back at his sister, obviously torn. "We'll wait out here, if you think you'll be okay."

"I'll be fine," she assured him. "I'm sorry to be such a pain."

He gave his sister a soft, affectionate smile that would have made Devin's knees go weak, if she weren't made of sterner stuff. "You're not a pain. You're just stubborn," he said gruffly. "You should have called me the minute you fell instead of waiting until I came back to the house and you definitely should have said something about the contractions."

"We'll take care of her and try to keep you posted."

"Thanks." He nodded and shepherded the two children to the small waiting room, with his sister's purse in hand.

Devin forced herself to put him out of her mind and focus on her patient.

Normally, the nurses and aides would take a patient into a room and start a chart but since she knew Tricia and the night was slow, Devin didn't mind coming into her care from the beginning.

"You're thirty-three weeks?" she asked as she pushed her into the largest exam room in the department.

"Almost thirty-four. Tuesday."

"With twins. Congratulations. Are they fraternal or identical?"

"Fraternal. A boy and a girl. The girl is measuring bigger, according to my ob-gyn back in California."

"Did your OB clear you for travel this close to your due date?"

"Yes. Everything has been uncomplicated. A textbook pregnancy, Dr. Adams said."

"When was your last appointment?"

"I saw my regular doctor the morning before Thanksgiving. She knew I was flying out to spend the holiday with Cole and the kids. I was supposed to be back the next Sunday, but, well, I decided to stay."

She paused and her chin started to quiver. "Everything is such a mess and I can't go home and now I've sprained my ankle. How am I going to get around on crutches when I'm as big as a barn?"

Something else was going on here, something that had nothing to do with sprained ankles. Why couldn't she go home? Devin squeezed her hand. "Let's not get ahead of ourselves."

"No. You're right." Tricia drew a breath. When she spoke her voice wobbled only a little. "I have an appointment Monday for a checkup with a local doctor. Randall or Crandall or something like that. I can't remember. I just know my records have been transferred there."

"Randall. Jim Randall."

He was one of her favorite colleagues in the area, compassionate and kind and more than competent. Whenever she had a complicated obstetrics patient in her family medicine practice, she sent her to Jim.

As Devin guided Tricia from the wheelchair to the narrow bed in the room, the pregnant woman paused on the edge, her hand curved around her abdomen and her face contorted with pain. She drew in a sharp breath and let it out slowly. "Ow. That was a big one."

And not far apart from the first contraction she'd had a few minutes earlier, Devin thought in concern, her priorities shifting as Callie came in. "Here we are. This is Callie. She's an amazing nurse and right now she's going to gather some basic information and help you into a gown. I'll be back when she's done to take a look at things."

Tricia grabbed her hand. "You'll be back?"

"In just a moment, I promise. I'm going to write orders for the X-ray and the fetal heartbeat monitoring and put a call in to Dr. Randall. I'll also order some basic urine and blood tests, too, then I'll be right back."

"Okay. Okay." Tricia gave a wobbly smile. "Thanks. I can't tell you how glad I am that you're here."

"I'm not going anywhere. I promise."

HE TRULY DETESTED HOSPITALS.

Cole shifted in the uncomfortable chair, his gaze on the little Christmas tree in the corner with its colorful lights and garland made out of rolled bandages.

Given the setting and the time of year, it was hard not to flash back to that miserable Christmas he was twelve, when his mother lay dying. That last week of her life, Stan had taken him and Tricia to the hospital just about every evening. They would sit in the waiting room near a pitiful little Christmas tree like this one and do homework or read or just gaze out the window at the falling snow in the moonlight, scared and sad and a little numb after months of their mother's chemotherapy and radiation.

He pushed away the memory, especially of all that came after, choosing instead to focus on the two good things that had come from hospitals: his kids, though he had only been there for Jazmyn's birth.

He could still remember walking through the halls and wanting to stop everybody there and share a drink with them and tell them about his beautiful new baby girl.

Emphasis on the part about sharing a drink. He sighed. By the time Sharla went into labor with Ty, things had been so terrible between them that she hadn't even told him the kid was on the way.

"I'm bored," the kid in question announced. "There's nothing to do."

Cole pointed to the small flat-screen TV hanging on the wall, showing some kind of talking heads on a muted news program. "Want to watch something? I'm sure we could find the remote somewhere. I can ask at the desk."

"I bet there's nothing on." Jazmyn slumped in her seat.

"Let's take a look. Maybe we could find a Christmas special or something."

Neither kid looked particularly enthusiastic but he headed over to the reception desk in search of a remote.

The woman behind the desk was a cute, curvy blonde with a friendly smile. Her name badge read Brittney and she had been watching him from under her fake eyelashes since he had filled out his sister's paperwork.

"Hi. Can I help you?" she asked.

"Hi, Brittney. I wonder if we can use the TV remote. My kids are getting a little restless."

"Oh. Sure. No prob." Her smile widened with a flirtatious look in her eyes. He'd like to think he was imagining it but he'd seen that look too many times from buckle bunnies on the rodeo circuit to mistake it for anything else.

He shifted, feeling self-conscious. A handful of years ago, he would have taken her up on the unspoken invitation in those big blue eyes. He would have done his best to tease out her phone number or would have made arrangements with her to meet up for a drink when her shift was over.

He might even have found a way to slip away with her on her next break to make out in a stairwell somewhere.

Though he had been a long, long time without a woman, he did his best to ignore the look. He hated the man he used to be and anything that reminded him of it.

"Thanks," he said stiffly when she handed over the remote. He took it from her and headed back to the kids.

"Here we go. Let's see what we can find."

He didn't have high hopes of finding a kids' show on at 7:00 p.m. on a Friday night but he was pleasantly surprised when the next click of the remote landed them on what looked like a stop-action animated holiday show featuring an elf, a snowman and a reindeer wearing a cowboy hat.

"How's this?" he asked.

"Okay," Ty said, agreeable as always.

"Looks like a little kids' show," Jazmyn said with a sniff but he noticed that after about two seconds, she was as interested in the action as her younger brother.

Jaz was quite a character, bossy and opinionated and domineering to her little brother and everyone else. How could he blame her for those sometimes annoying traits, which she had likely developed from being forced into little mother mode for her brother most of the time and even for their mother if Sharla was going through a rough patch?

He leaned back in the chair and wished he had a cowboy hat like the reindeer so he could yank it down over his face, stretch out his boots and take a rest for five freaking minutes.

Between the ranch and the kids and now Tricia, he felt stretched to the breaking point.

Tricia. What was he supposed to do with her? A few weeks ago, he thought she was only coming for Thanksgiving. The kids, still lost and grieving and trying to settle into their new routine with him, showed unusual excitement at the idea of seeing their aunt from California, the one who showered them with presents and cards.

She had assured him her doctor said she was fine to travel. Over their Skype conversation, she had given him a bright smile and told him she wanted to come out while she still could. Her husband was on a business trip, she told him, and she didn't want to spend Thanksgiving on her own.

How the hell was he supposed to have figured out she was running away?

He sighed. His life had seemed so much less complicated two months ago.

He couldn't say it had ever been *uncomplicated*, but he had found a groove the past few years. His world consisted of the ranch, his child support payments, regular check-ins with his parole officer and the biweekly phone calls and occasional visits to wherever Sharla in her wanderlust called home that week so he could stay in touch with his kids.

He had tried to keep his head down and throw everything he had into making Evergreen Springs and his horse training operation a success, to create as much order as he could out of the chaos his selfish and stupid mistakes had caused.

Two months ago, everything had changed. First had come a call from his ex-wife. She and her current boyfriend were heading to Reno for a week to get married—her second since their stormy marriage ended just months after Ty's birth—and Sharla wanted him to meet her in Boise so he could pick up the kids.

Forget that both kids had school or that Cole was supposed to be at a horse show in Denver that weekend.

He had dropped everything, relishing the rare chance to be with his kids without more of Sharla's drama. He had wished his ex-wife well, shook hands with the new guy—who actually had seemed like a decent sort, for a change—and sent them on their way.

Only a few days later, he received a second phone call, one that would alter his life forever.

He almost hadn't been able to understand Sharla's mother, Trixie, when she called. In between all the sobbing and wailing and carrying on, he figured out the tragic and stunning news that the newlyweds had been killed after their car slid out of control during an early snowstorm while crossing the Sierra Nevada.

In a moment, everything changed. For years, Cole had been fighting for primary custody, trying to convince judge after judge that their mother's flighty, unstable lifestyle and periodic substance abuse provided a terrible environment for the children.

The only trouble was, Cole had plenty of baggage of his own. An ex-con former alcoholic didn't exactly have the sturdiest leg to stand on when it came to being granted custody of two young children, no matter how much he had tried to rebuild his life and keep his nose out of trouble in recent years.

Sharla's tragic death changed everything and Cole now had full custody of his children as the surviving parent.

It hadn't been an easy transition for any of them, complicated by the fact that he'd gone through two housekeepers in as many months.

Now he had his sister to take care of. Whether her ankle was broken or sprained, the result would be more domestic chaos.

He would figure it out. He always did, right? What other choice did he have?

He picked up a *National Geographic* and tried to find something to read to keep himself awake. He was deep in his third article and the kids onto their second Christmas special before the lovely doctor returned.

She was every bit as young as he had thought at first, pretty and petite with midlength auburn hair, green eyes that were slightly almond shaped and porcelain skin. She even had a little smattering of freckles across the bridge of her nose. Surely she was too young to be in such a responsible position.

He rose, worry for his sister crowding out everything else.

"How is she? Is her ankle broken? How are the babies?"

"You were right to bring her in. I'm sorry things have been taking so long. It must be almost the children's bedtime."

"They're doing okay for now. How is Tricia?"

Dr. Shaw gestured to the chair and sat beside him after he sank back down. That was never a good sign, when the doctor took enough time to sit down, too.

"For the record, she gave me permission to share information with you. I can tell you that she has a severe sprain from the fall. I've called our orthopedics specialist on call and he's taking a look at her now to figure out a treatment plan. With the proper brace, her ankle should heal in a month or so. She'll have to stay off it for a few weeks, which means a wheelchair."

His mind raced through the possible implications of that. He needed to find a housekeeper immediately. He had three new green broke horses coming in the next few days for training and he was going to be stretched thin over the next few weeks—lousy timing over the holidays, but he couldn't turn down the work when he was trying so hard to establish Evergreen Springs as a powerhouse training facility.

How would he do everything on his own? Why couldn't things ever be easy?

"The guest room and bathroom are both on the main level," he said. "That will help. Can we pick up the wheelchair here or do I have to go somewhere else to find one?"

The doctor was silent for a few beats too long and he gave her a careful look.

"What aren't you telling me?" he asked.

She released a breath. "Your sister also appears to be in the beginning stages of labor."

He stared. "It's too early! The babies have to be too small."

Panic and guilt bloomed inside him, ugly and dark, and he rose, restless with all the emotions teeming inside him. She shouldn't have been outside where she risked falling. He *told* her she didn't have to go out to the bus to pick up the children. The stop was only a few hundred yards from the front door. They could walk up themselves, he told her, but she insisted on doing it every day. Said she needed the fresh air and the exercise.

Now look where they were.

Don't miss
EVERGREEN SPRINGS by RaeAnne Thayne,
available October 2015 wherever
Harlequin HQN books and ebooks are sold.
www.Harlequin.com

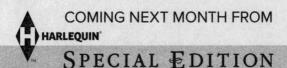

REQUEST YOUR FREE BOOKS!

2 FREE NOVELS PLUS 2 FREE GIFTS!

SPECIAL EDITION

Life, Love & Family

YES! Please send me 2 FREE Harlequin® Special Edition novels and my 2 FREE gifts (gifts are worth about $10). After receiving them, if I don't wish to receive any more books, I can return the shipping statement marked "cancel." If I don't cancel, I will receive 6 brand-new novels every month and be billed just $4.74 per book in the U.S. or $5.49 per book in Canada. That's a savings of at least 12% off the cover price! It's quite a bargain! Shipping and handling is just 50¢ per book in the U.S. and 75¢ per book in Canada.* I understand that accepting the 2 free books and gifts places me under no obligation to buy anything. I can always return a shipment and cancel at any time. Even if I never buy another book, the two free books and gifts are mine to keep forever.

235/335 HDN GH3Z

Name _____ (PLEASE PRINT)

Address _____ Apt. #

City _____ State/Prov. _____ Zip/Postal Code

Signature (if under 18, a parent or guardian must sign)

Mail to the **Reader Service:**
IN U.S.A.: P.O. Box 1867, Buffalo, NY 14240-1867
IN CANADA: P.O. Box 609, Fort Erie, Ontario L2A 5X3

Want to try two free books from another line?
Call 1-800-873-8635 or visit www.ReaderService.com.

* Terms and prices subject to change without notice. Prices do not include applicable taxes. Sales tax applicable in N.Y. Canadian residents will be charged applicable taxes. Offer not valid in Quebec. This offer is limited to one order per household. Not valid for current subscribers to Harlequin Special Edition books. All orders subject to credit approval. Credit or debit balances in a customer's account(s) may be offset by any other outstanding balance owed by or to the customer. Please allow 4 to 6 weeks for delivery. Offer available while quantities last.

Your Privacy—The Reader Service is committed to protecting your privacy. Our Privacy Policy is available online at www.ReaderService.com or upon request from the Reader Service.

We make a portion of our mailing list available to reputable third parties that offer products we believe may interest you. If you prefer that we not exchange your name with third parties, or if you wish to clarify or modify your communication preferences, please visit us at www.ReaderService.com/consumerchoice or write to us at Reader Service Preference Service, P.O. Box 9062, Buffalo, NY 14240-9062. Include your complete name and address.

"Everything's okay, Abby. Really."

"No, it's not." Clenching her hands, she took a step
into the room.

"Abby?" he questioned.

"I don't know if I'm being a fool. I was a fool once
before."

Rory nodded, but didn't try to persuade her.

"You could have any woman in the world," she said,
her voice cracking.

"I don't want any woman in the world." The answer
was quiet and firm. "And I sure as hell don't want to make
your life any harder. I should have kept my mouth shut."

"No." She was glad he hadn't, because in addition
to the simmering desire he woke in her, she felt a new
glowing kernel, one that seemed to be emerging from the
destruction Porter had left in his wake. A sense of self, of
worth. Just a kernel, but Rory McLane had brought that
back to life.

"You…" She trailed off, unsure what to say. Then, "You make me feel like a woman again."

The smallest, gentlest of smiles curved his lips. "I'm glad."

"I don't know if this is smart. No promises."

"None," he agreed. "Maybe that's not good for you."

"Maybe that's exactly what I need."

His brows lifted. "How so?"

"Just to be. Just to feel like a woman. Just to know I can please…"

"Aw, hell." He crossed the room and pulled her up against him, the skin of his chest warm and smooth against her cheek. "You please me. Already you please me. Are you sure?"

She managed a jerky nod. She was sure she needed this experience. She wasn't sure how she'd feel about it tomorrow, but she *had* to know if she could make a man happy in bed. Porter had stripped that from her, and damn it, she wanted it back.

And more than anything else she wanted Rory. Just once. It was like a child's plea. *Let me just once.*

But it was no child leaning into him, lifting her arms to wrap them around his narrow waist. It was a woman trying to be born again.